THE ROT

PAUL KANE

First published in 2016 by
Horrific Tales Publishing
http://www.horrifictales.co.uk

A CIP catalogue record for this book is available from the British Library

ISBN: 978-1-910283-16-5

INTRODUCTION
BY
TIM LEBBON

There is a fine tradition amongst writers for destroying the world. You can't blame us. It's a fun thing to do, and sometimes the world feels like it needs destroying. Just to see what comes next. Just to see how those few who manage to survive move on into whatever brave new world might evolve out of humanity's decline and eventual extinction.

And to see how little effect our passing will really have on Planet Earth.

I've always been fascinated with the End of All Things. I've destroyed the world a lot of times in my fiction - too many to bother counting - and I've killed literally billions of people, often in pretty horrible ways. I've nuked them, poisoned them, had them eaten by nasty beasties, served them up as a zombie feast, frozen them to death, drowned them, burned them, and melted them down into a haze of nano-techy things. I'm often asked why I write so much apocalyptic fiction (to be fair, probably only 5% of what I've written has been apocalyptic, if that...but people tend to remember the world being destroyed). I always take a stab at answering, but in truth it never feels quite right. I don't know for sure what the fascination is...but I suspect it's to do with the final death.

Lots of horror fiction is about death - confronting it, experiencing it, dealing with it, or not. Apocalyptic fiction is about the death of Us, not just the death of One. One day Humanity will go, whether it's in a brief blaze of cosmic fire, or a whimper of burned or diseased bodies. Writing about that is a way of exploring not only what it is to be human, but what it is to be humanity. We're barely a flicker in universal memory. Cold, dark infinity doesn't care about us. As Richard Dawkins said, "Nature is neither kind nor cruel, but pitilessly indifferent." It doesn't matter *at all* to the universe whether we as a species live or die.

Which leaves it up to us to make the choice.

Apocalyptic fiction is about our struggle for survival against universal indifference. Whether it's individual survival or survival as a species, we're fighting against that cold dark infinity as it tries to swallow us up.

What would you do to survive? What *wouldn't* you do? How far would you go?

I can't remember the first apocalyptic novel I read. I suspect it was *The Day of the Triffids* (Wyndham's novels are still among the best). It quickly led on to many more, and sometime in my mid-teens I read the novel which remains one of my favourites to this day. *The Stand* by Stephen King is a mighty work (both in scope and physical heft!), and it set the benchmark for the many apocalyptic novels to follow. Other favourites of mine include *The Death of Grass* by John Christopher, *World War Z* by Max Brooks, *Swan Song* by Robert McCammon, *The Purple Cloud* by M. P. Shiel, *War of the Worlds* by H. G. Wells, and many, many more.

In *The Rot*, Paul Kane takes the apocalypse and makes it all his own, adding to the roster of splendid horrors we all love to fear. This novella really is a grim slice of horror. I guess you could call it science fiction, but really it's so bloody, gritty, and *meaty*, that edging it towards the SF realm would probably be misleading. There are a couple of original sciency ideas that are interesting, but make no mistake - this is a horror story.

It's difficult writing an introduction to a work like this without giving away some of what makes it such a compelling read. But one of the aspects I liked so much -

and which I think is an idea that could easily be visited again by Paul - was the SKIN. The concept of this futuristic creation is both neat and simple. The SKIN is a high-tech body covering that helps protect and maintain the wearer for an indefinite amount of time. It'll recycle body waste, from the obvious examples, to shed hair and skin, blood, and all the other nasties you can imagine. It'll filter out any dangers from outside, such as viruses and bacteria. It will even seal and treat minor wounds suffered by the wearer.

In effect, the SKIN is a barrier between the protagonist and the rest of the world, both physical and, more importantly, psychological. He's one step removed from the world around him - cut off, effectively, from everything he has always known - even though he still exists within it. This is the idea I found most interesting. He wanders through the slowly degenerating world like a ghost, interacting yet still protected (to some extent) from the decline that has settled into the world he knows and loves. He's suffered loss, and is destined to suffer more, but as the novella progresses he tries to shake the idea that he's simply an observer, and become part of the world once again.

The story is told in a very conversational style. It's informal and comfortable, and even quite light-hearted during the opening paragraphs, and that's misleading, because *The Rot* is far from that. It's like listening to someone chatting over a pint about cutting off your head and gouging out your heart. That's intentional, because the whole story is written as the protagonist's recorded version of events. I'll be honest, it took a few pages for me to get used to this style. But once it hit home what it meant - a first-person, last person's testimony - I think it worked extremely well. I like first person narratives anyway (as a writer as much as a reader) because it often makes a story more immediate, and more satisfying when you're trying to get inside a character's head. It works exceptionally well here, and as a reader you start to feel just as trapped as the protagonist, in his head, in his SKIN.

Then there's the idea itself. I don't want to say too much about it, because it grows and expands in clever and shocking ways throughout the novella (although the title will give you a pretty good idea of what you're letting yourself in for). But it's a good one, and I don't remember reading a concept exactly like this before in horror fiction. There's a hopelessness to the protagonist's plight, a grimness hanging over his every word all the way through the story. Sometimes such grimness can be overly cloying, but that's not the case here. His striving to move on, to discover more, to find a way back, is even more traumatic in the face of what he's facing.

Besides, I like grim stories. They can get down to the deep, dark depths of a character's soul, and strip them bare. In *The Rot*, confusion leads to stunned understanding, hope is presented and then ripped away again, and grim inevitability sings through behind the protagonist's conversational tone. I loved it from beginning to end.

Tim Lebbon

Goytre, South Wales

August 2016.

THE ROT

Paul Kane

For Jon, David and all at Abaddon/Rebellion – feeding my post-apocalyptic writing habit for almost a decade.

‘Change and decay in all around I see.’

Abide with Me.

CHAPTER ONE

Record:

Testing, testing, 1, 2, 3. Mary had a little... Okay, enough of that shit.

Pause. Playback.

Resume recording:

Right, seems to be working. Captain's Log, Stardate... No, not even funny. Not now we won't even get to it, won't see that future since the world's gone to... Have to stay positive, there's always hope; that's what Mum always used to say, before... Might be a way to reverse all this, I just have to find it. Getting off topic, need to start from the beginning. In the beginning, there was the word - and that word was *fucked*. Again, not funny. Need to set all this down for someone - even if it's just me. Can't use paper and pen, can't use computers - this is the only way. To be honest, I'd totally forgotten the SKIN had this facility. Yeah, I mean, I read the handbook, sort of, listened to the lectures - though a lot of it went over my head, I'll admit. But given more time, I'd have got a handle on it. I did remember eventually, so that's got to count for something, right? It's not like I haven't been busy, but I prefer to be active, y'know? Always have. Act, then look back on things later - so I guess it's pretty apt that I haven't started to use this until a couple of months after everything...

Jesus, has it really only been two months? All right, closer to three. It's like being a kid again, holidays with all those weeks stretching out ahead of you. Seemed to last a lifetime, playing outside in the sun, trips to parks and the seaside. Then when you grow up everything goes by so much quicker; you work, you don't stop to smell the roses -

you take it all for granted. Not like when you're little, everything's an exploration, everything's wondrous. The simplest of things, like kicking a ball around on a patch of wasteland becomes magical. Time, since it all happened, *has* slowed down, like the summer holidays when I was small. There's been nothing wondrous about any of this, though, nothing to marvel at. Only a longing for how things were before. But you can't go back. I don't think I even... No, I didn't appreciate what was left when it still was there. When things were whole. Like I say, I was too busy.

Busy trying to stay alive mostly.

I shouldn't really *be* alive anyway - I mean, I haven't eaten anything in all that time or had anything to drink. Not really. The SKIN's kept me going, but I feel like a ghost drifting through this new world sometimes. Like I don't really exist... until something happens and I realise that actually, yes, I do - and there are so many dangers, so many things that could happen to me that would turn me into the real thing. A ghost... or worse, one of *them*. Right, I know what you're thinking, how can I be talking to you now when I haven't eaten a scrap of food or taken a drink in so, so long. I know the facts and figures: you can manage about three weeks without food. Without water, you'll only last three days. And I can't help thinking about Mum when I think about all this, surviving on that drip because she'd forgotten how to eat - fucking dementia - until they pulled the plug, that was. "It's cruel to keep her alive like this," the doctors told us, "it's artificial." So they'd disconnected her. We'd tried to feed her, spoon-fed her yoghurts, but she wouldn't have any of it - and in the end she just shrivelled up, a tiny husk like a mummy in that hospital bed. We spent three days just waiting, me, my Dad and Aunty Pat - three days waiting and holding her hand, saying prayers that were never answered. But I tell you what, she fought - good Christ did she fight to hold on to life, to hope, right up to the last breath.

I take after her, I reckon; I've got her stubbornness.

Dad went on for five years after that. Killed himself, because he was diagnosed with terminal cancer. Those were the big two weren't they, dementia and cancer. The two diseases we were struggling so hard to fight, until... These we thought, naively, were the ones which would finish us off as a race. Can't say I blame him for the choice he made, he'd seen enough of what happened to Mum as she wasted away; he just gave in. Neighbours realised that his milk was piling up outside and called the authorities, who smashed down the door to find the empty pill box next to him, his body slumped over the couch. He'd been there for the same amount of time we'd spent in the hospital... I didn't see him until the funeral, and by then the undertakers had done their work - and I remember thinking there was nothing more artificial than that. I can imagine what he must have looked like when they found him, having now seen so much of it first-hand.

Doesn't do any good to think about that, though. What's the point?

How did I come to be talking about it anyway? Oh right, the SKIN - how it kept me alive. Even more artificial. In a word: recyc. It's been doing that since day one, taking the last meal and the last drink ever to pass my lips, taking the waste from that, and using it, breaking it all down into the bare minimum needed to nourish me - then feeding that back into my body. Don't ask me to explain the ins and outs - ha! - because they're above my paygrade, not that I have a paygrade anymore. Beyond my understanding then, shall we say. Something the eggheads cooked up in their research and development labs - and sometimes I thank them for that, though other times I want to spit on their graves; if I could spit anywhere, that is. It's also a prototype, the first and - as far as I'm aware - only one in existence, unless similar suits were being worked on in other parts of the world, of course. You should have seen the number of forms I had to sign before I was even allowed into that place, let alone told about the SKIN. Wanted my first born and everything.

The endless dreams I've had about that last meal – that last supper – they gave me. Steak, potatoes, veg, everything the body could possibly need – washed down with water. No beer, no whisky; couldn't poison myself before the experiment began, you see. I even had to have a detox a couple of weeks before I was taken to the facility. All part of the purification process. Although you wouldn't necessarily be completely "pure" if you had cause to use the SKIN, they needed *me* to be a baseline. It was only intended to be a week anyway, that first lot of tests, but things didn't exactly pan out that way, as you'll probably already know if you're listening to this. If there's nobody left in the future to listen, then, well... Let's not go there. Let's assume there's still hope. Let's show a little of Mum's fighting spirit, shall we, Adam?

Oh, that's a point – I haven't said who I am yet, have I? My name's Adam Keller. I'm not a captain, but I am a lieutenant. A former flight lieutenant in fact... and a test pilot. There's nothing I like better than to be up in those clouds, preferably at breakneck speeds – though that was how I had my little accident in the first place. Not my first, of course, but the one that grounded me – at least as far as my Queen and country were concerned. Months in hospital, leg pinned; a regular bionic man. After that, I was fit enough, just not fit to test planes that flew at those kinds of speeds. Up until that happened, I was on a fast track to possibly representing my country up there, out in the Final Frontier, or a Galaxy Far, Far Away, depending on your preference. Instead, I wound up being a professional guinea pig, test 'piloting' everything apart from the planes I loved so much. Couldn't really complain, it paid well – especially under-the-counter stuff.

Oddly, I felt the closest to my once-cherished goals of space exploration by testing the SKIN. It's what it was originally developed for – not just inhospitable environments on this planet, but others as well. A survival suit. It's right there in the name, right at the start: Survivor's Kinetic Integrated Network. S.K.I.N. A *second* skin, powered by your own movement – was how it was described to me by that nice Dr Weeks. Reminded me a little of Stan Laurel from those old black and white movies, he did. I imagined that the slightest harsh word would make him bawl his eyes out... Oh, right. On point. A second skin, one that would adapt to protect against the cold, from disease and toxins, filter out impurities in the air - even make air that was previously unbreathable safe for human consumption - and keep a person ticking along indefinitely. Or until help arrived in the form of a rescue mission, say.

Personally, I'm not holding my breath. - that's even now, as I speak, being filtered by the tiny, microscopic robots that work so hard on my behalf. Most of the time, I even forget they're there, covering my entire naked body, giving me a weird shimmering appearance if you get too close - which I daresay wouldn't hurt with regards to that ghostly metaphor - although a better description would probably be that it's like a fish's scales. But - and I hadn't thought about it till just now, until I started talking about rescue missions - there are still people up there, out in space, that haven't been affected by all this. That might find my recordings. Do they even know what's happened, I wonder, or did radio communication just go dead on them? They should probably just stay up there, because one thing's for damned sure, if they come back down to Earth it's going to be with a bump - whatever their landing's like. They're going to find it a much-changed place; going to be in for a shock when they see what's happened to—

Bear with me, I'm not great at this. I never kept a diary when I was a kid, was never much for the social-media craze that swept the world back in the day and never really went away again, only got worse and worse. Always found it hard enough to talk to other people in person, let alone by electronic means. This is different, though - this is important. This is something that needs reporting; that's worth chronicling, even if it's only fucking aliens that find it in thousands of years' time.

Not my great escape, although I will get to that in a second, but everything afterwards. I'll try and keep this...

what, journal?... try and keep it up to date. I figure if nothing else, it might just stop me from going stark, staring mad. Hold on, let me just see if—

Stop. Playback.

Resume recording:

God, what a complete and utter wanker I sound. Samuel Pepys I am not, but I'm all there is, so tough shit.

Too easily distracted, too random. I'll try to keep it on track now and get through what happened at the facility first of all. Try not to bore anyone with my reminiscences about my folks, about life before all this. It's just that I can't help thinking back. Can't help wishing that—

The facility. Okay, picture this: I'm taken there in the middle of the night, only allowed to pack a few essential items, I'm told - won't need them anyway. Ain't that the truth? Thankfully, I'm not really a sentimental kind of guy - my small flat's quite bare. I'm also a 'travel light' type of person, always have been. Goes back not only to my time in the armed services, but also the travelling I did in my late teens. Backpacking mainly, staying in hostels or just camping out. Saw most of the world that way, and what I didn't I saw when I joined up. Not going off topic again, it's relevant I promise... Right, right. The facility. I was picked up by a dark 4x4, all very *Men in Black*, and we drove for a good few hours. After the first hour I began to notice fewer and fewer buildings, as we wound our way up and down country lanes.

So there we were, out in the middle of nowhere and away from prying eyes, and as dawn broke over the horizon we came up on our destination. Well, we came up on the fencing surrounding it - electrified I was guessing, and patrolled by guards in navy jumpsuits with guns and Alsatians. At the gate, IDs were checked and I was even palm-printed. Then we drove through the grounds and I got my first clear view of the facility itself. There were maybe a dozen storeys to it, and I thought I saw the edge of a rotor on the roof; some kind of landing pad? Then we parked up outside, slotting in beside the other cars that presumably belonged to staff. The same level of security continued inside here, as several armed men greeted us. You'd be forgiven for thinking that Blofeld was inside, cooking up his diabolical schemes, but there was only Weeks - who was the head of this particular programme. I got the impression it was his baby and he was very proud of it; had every right to be, as it turned out.

After saying our hellos, I was whisked up in a lift to a mid-level floor - judging from the numbers - the one where the SKIN was being developed and would be put through its paces. Wasn't a large floor, just a few rooms and corridors, including a place where I could eat and a room to billet in until they were ready to begin the tests. Not the tests on the suit, oh no - first came round after round of medical examinations, a lot of them conducted by Weeks and a nurse. I never did catch her name, but I caught the way she looked at me when she didn't think I was taking any notice. She was pretty, that woman - long tawny hair tied up in a bun, kind eyes behind her glasses. The kind of girl I could have seen myself with; no attachments - just something fun, y'know?

I've never been great with relationships; comes from not being great with people full stop. So the women I'd been with in the past, once I'd gotten over that awkward first hurdle, didn't tend to be anything more than casual flings. And when I say 'casual', I don't mean I took any risks in *that* department. I was careful.

This is probably not something I should be talking about in a historical document, is it? Like I said, no Sammy Pepys.

Didn't know her name, but then who was to say Weeks was the doctor's real name? It's all cloak and dagger with these guys, but I could respect that. I don't tend to shove my nose into business that doesn't concern me, and I know when to keep my mouth shut, which is probably what got me most of these gigs in the first place. This one I figured I could do standing on my head, once I'd been given the option of whether to go through with it or back out. Sitting on my arse reading or watching TV, playing vid-games in a sealed off room to see whether this new suit they were talking about worked in different environments? Piece of cake, I said to myself. Then they told me about the other stuff.

First there was the fact they were going to shave me completely, they'd left that off the job description - something to do with conductivity. SKIN on skin. Wouldn't grow back either, as long as I was wearing it. I swallowed that. After all, it wouldn't be forever and I was getting paid enough. Then there was the big one.

"It's going to do what?" I asked.

"In layman's terms," Weeks said to me, "it'll take your waste and reprocess it on a loop, to sustain your body."

"I'm going to be eating my own shit, is that what you're telling me? Drinking my own—"

Weeks held up his hand and shook his head at the same time. "I wouldn't have put it so crudely myself, and it will be more like you are absorbing the processed nutrients than eating - once the SKIN is covering you completely, you won't be able to eat or drink anything in the way that you normally do. Look, you really don't have to worry about all that."

"Oh, *don't* I?" I replied.

"It's not harmful in any way, I assure you," Weeks insisted. "Please, Lieutenant Keller..."

If I'd pushed the point I think the tears would have come and Weeks would've started scratching at the top of his head. But I sighed, shook my head, and signed the releases, thinking it probably sounded worse than it was. In all honesty, it does - you don't even really notice what's happening mostly; like any other 'natural' function, only it's being taken care of by the SKIN rather than you. And, like I say, it was only going to be for a little while at a time; a week for starters. It'd go quickly enough with stuff to entertain me – I'm a slow reader, so one e-book would probably see me right, though there were thousands on the tablet they gave me. I could catch up on some of those classics I'd never got around to checking out, like *Moby Dick*; you know, the one where that sailor was chasing the whale. *War and Peace*, stuff like that. Stuff that... well, I don't think is going to be around now in years to come. Maybe not even in months to come.

Wish I'd got around to them, but sadly I started in on the vid-games and movies first and never got to the books. Three days I was in there, just three days – I knew because of the calendar-clock on the wall. Something quite appropriate about that. Made it to the halfway mark, sitting there in the SKIN – though they had allowed me some dignity, a pair of shorts over the top of it so I wouldn't be completely in the altogether; that and a pair of boots. Weeks and his team, especially the nurse, had seen everything I'd got anyway doing their prodding and poking. Just a shred of human decency; something to make me more comfortable, I suppose. Wasn't to keep me warm either, as they reduced the heat in there; the SKIN would maintain a neutral body temperature at all times. They'd told me that in all the briefings about the suit, gone through everything until my eyes had started to glaze over. Including the digital recorder... but that went out of my head altogether until a few hours ago, as I said. Wasn't expected to make comments about how the trial was going, that was their job – they were checking and recording, even observing in person through that huge window. Felt a bit like I was in an interrogation room from some cheesy cop show at times – only it wasn't a two-way mirror – or like a rat in a lab being scrutinised... yeah, more like that.

I was a lab rat; had been for a long while.

Occasionally I played a few hands of cards with one of the sentries that had been posted on that level – he'd be sitting on one side of the glass, me on the other. Not only helped pass the time, but made it all feel less... peculiar. I also slept - a lot. I was asleep when it all hit the fan, actually; curled up on that camp bed when the sirens started. I have no idea who hit them, especially knowing what I do now; maybe they were automated? Anyway, took me a minute or so to remember exactly where I was. Thought for a moment there I was back on my travels as a teenager, in a tent in some foreign land.

Then I heard the gunfire.

That roused me, got me on my feet pretty fucking quickly I can tell you. Because it was close, and getting closer. It was machine-gun fire, machine guns like the ones I'd seen the guards carrying. My first thought was that somebody was trying to break in, perhaps to steal the SKIN? They'd caught wind of it and wanted to either copy the thing or make a fortune selling the tech on the black market. Didn't matter that it hadn't been properly tested yet - that I was in the process of doing that right now - it would still have gone for several million to the right buyer. People like that would probably rip it off me, and they wouldn't want to leave any witnesses.

Then he was there, walking backwards holding the rifle: a modified Heckler & Koch MP5 with scope, to be exact. Not the guard I'd played poker with, but another one wearing the same navy jumpsuit and beret they all had on. The only way I could tell them apart was the colour of their hair; this one blond, a bit lighter than my own shade. He was backing into the stretch of corridor facing my room, then he suddenly began firing his weapon again. Short bursts, his teeth gritted.

"What? What is it?" I shouted through the glass. "What..."

I stepped away sharply when he turned, facing me with a look I'll never forget as long as I live. The clenched teeth - what I'd taken for panic, fear, something I'd seen all too often in combat - was accompanied by a wide-eyed expression that told me he was anything but frightened. It was manic, wild, and more than a little terrifying to actually look at - like the Joker, but less controlled. A faint line of saliva ran from the corner of his mouth as he cocked his head and stared at me. I'd never felt more like a lab rat than in that moment, or maybe some sort of larger animal that was this man's prey. He raised the gun, and I wondered then if the glass was bullet-proof. Why would it be? There was no reason *for* it to be, so probably not. In any event, I was about to find out one way or another.

I'd also assumed, wrongly, that the gunfire had been two way - the guard defending himself against an enemy - but I saw now, as one of the white-coated technicians entered the frame, that he was shooting at unarmed people. His attention diverted by the young man making a grab for his weapon, the blond sentry turned and pressed the trigger. The techie danced about for a moment or two, the bullets being pumped into him keeping the guy in the air, before he was thrown back against the far wall - leaving a smear of bright redness in his wake as he slumped down it. It stood out more than it probably should have, that trail of crimson, because of the starkness of the wall; the clothes he'd been wearing were no longer white, but saturated with the colour. The whole thing looked like some sort of horrific modern art exhibit.

But the guard wasn't finished yet.

It was clear the man was dead, sitting there in a pool of his own blood; one leg bent underneath him; both hands turned upwards like a beggar waiting for a handout; head lolling on his chest. Or at least it was before the guard took hold of it by the hair, gripping and yanking it back until it rested there against the wall.

I saw what was about to happen, screamed, "No, *don't!*" I'm not entirely sure why, because the techie was already dead. Maybe it was that humanity thing again, that gut reaction telling you this shouldn't be happening - that nobody should be doing the things he was doing.

He then proceeded to shoot into that head, more bullets

striking it at point blank range. The effect was like a melon being hit repeatedly with a bat, until there was nothing you could really call a head anymore – just the tattered stump of a neck. His rifle clicked on empty, and for that I was grateful. Only he ejected the mag and reloaded, slamming in another full one from his pocket – an automatic action he must have done a thousand times.

"Christ," I said under my breath. I knew I had to get out of there, but when I went to the door and tried it, nothing happened. *"Christ!"* I said again, louder this time, perhaps thinking that he was the only one who might be able to help me now. It was clear what had happened, a lone nutter had gone apeshit for whatever reason – you see it on the news all the time; pressures of work, his home life, addiction to something... – usually gambling, which affected all the others – and was shooting up the place. Shooting up the folk who worked there, too. Didn't know when to *stop* shooting, in fact. Couldn't even see when his bullets were no longer hitting flesh.

Case in point, he was already pressing the trigger as he turned back in my direction; suddenly remembering what he'd been about to do before the techie interrupted him. The fish in a certain barrel – or bowl might be more accurate – he needed to put down. Luckily, this time – because I'd moved towards the door – I was able to duck, spread myself across the floor as the bullets hit the glass. I covered my head with my hands, though what protection that would give me I had no idea – they'd just end up like that poor sod's bonce. As it turned out, I didn't need protection anyway. When I risked a glance up, I saw that the glass was scratched, but holding. *Looks like it* is *toughened after all*, I thought.

The guard cocked his head again and opened his mouth – this time a cascade of drool poured out. It was foaming, like he'd been bitten by a dog with rabies. Could that be the explanation? Had one of those Alsatians I'd seen done this? Right at that moment, did it even matter? I had more pressing things to worry about... The glass was being weakened by the hail of bullets still bombarding it - not even the reinforced stuff would hold out forever. Then the noise stopped; sorry, the *firing* stopped... because the alarms were still going.

The guard dropped his gun on the ground next to the window, suddenly reaching up, reaching around, clawing at his back. He spun, chasing whatever was behind him that I couldn't see...and then suddenly I could. The man had a fire-axe planted squarely in the middle of his back, the wood dangling uselessly down from its head. His fingers continued to reach for the thing with little success. Someone had done it, stopped this prick in his tracks - stopped his rampage before he could get to me. And I thought then about the poor techie who hadn't been so fortunate. Then I thought, *how many more are out there in that same condition?* A few? Dozens? Might have murdered everyone in the entire fucking building for all I knew. Hadn't got us all, though. Hadn't got me, and hadn't got whoever had done the number on him with the axe.

As he fell, the guard dropped to his knees and revealed my saviour. Imagine my surprise when I saw that it was Dr Weeks, who always looked like he wouldn't say boo to a goose. Well, he'd do more than say boo it seemed; would lop the thing in two as soon as look at it. Weeks was gaping down at the guard, admiring his handiwork as the man toppled over sideways, still unable to dislodge the weapon. Except Weeks was crying, looking more like Stan Laurel than ever with his face crumpled up like that. I wanted to go to him then, tell him he'd done the right thing - the *only* thing, given the circumstances. Lord knows how many more lives he'd saved by taking down that maniac.

But there was something about the tears, something about the way his face was contorting. There was no sadness there, not really. And as he began to laugh, I saw that same look of insanity wash over his features... just before he retrieved the axe and set to work on the rest of the guard, swinging it like he was a lumberjack chopping up a pine. At one point it got stuck in the guy's side, so

Weeks put his foot on the body - holding it in place so he could wrench out the axe. I watched all this slack-jawed, unable to look away. It was almost as shocking as what I'd seen the guard do, and even more unexpected.

Then suddenly he was done. Weeks met my gaze, the tears still streaming down his face, and he howled. I swear to God he actually howled... like it was the full moon or something and he was about to go native. Was that it? Had the dog that infected the guard bitten Weeks as well?

But the howl turned into a laugh, then wracking sobs - before he ran at the glass, head-butting it over and over again. Head-butting it until there were more red smears, this time on the glass, and he'd joined the guard on the floor. It was only then that I rose to a crouching position, before standing upright. I walked towards the glass, but still couldn't take my eyes off the scene in front of me. My vision was flitting between the bodies of the guard, the techie, then back to Weeks and his damaged head.

What the fuck... just *what* the actual fuck?

Eventually, I tried the door again, but still couldn't get it to open. It was electronic, so maybe when the alarms kicked in everything shut down, I reasoned. That just left one way out...

I went back to the window, pressed on the glass with my fingertips. Then I banged on it, testing again - this time for weak spots in the surface. And let me tell you, it was still pretty solid, even after everything. I stood there banging on it with my fist, even kicked it a few times - not even thinking back then that I might damage the SKIN, might make a tear in it that could... Fortunately, it's a tough son of a bitch too, this stuff I'm cocooned in. It's had to be over these past few months.

I tried with chairs and my camp bed next, kicking myself for not thinking of it sooner. I swung them at the glass, but still nothing happened; maybe if I'd had Weeks' axe, which was just out of reach... I gave up a few times, sat down and waited for someone else to come along - someone sane. At some point during this, the alarms had ceased their wailing as well, for which I was thankful. Finally, I got up and tried again, one last attempt - feeling it give around the spot where Weeks had been throwing himself at the pane. It splintered, spider-webbing from the centre outwards, weakening it more and more.

One last swing with the chair did it, and the glass shattered, then fell like rain onto the floor - both inside and outside the room. I stepped out cautiously, mainly because I had no idea what might be waiting for me around the corner, but also due to the fact there was so much blood everywhere. As I peered around the bend, I saw more of it leading up the corridor. Could have just been from the guard's exploits, but I stooped to pick up his MP5 anyway... and took his pistol from the holster as well - just for good measure - tucking that into the back of my shorts.

I'd only taken a couple of steps down that corridor when I sensed someone behind me. I turned just in time to see Weeks coming at me with the axe. Somehow he'd survived the beating he'd inflicted on himself - don't ask me how, because his head was one big wound, redness dripping from cuts in his forehead and rolling down his cheeks like *bloody* tears now. Had just been unconscious rather than dead. And now he was taking up his old hobbies with the axe, except I was the target.

I dodged sideways and the weapon missed me by inches, embedding itself in the wall behind. All that time in my room I'd been wanting it, and now the damned thing had nearly taken my head off. Weeks hissed at me, before pulling back and freeing the axe's head. I began backing away, rifle raised. "Don't make me do this, Doc," I said to him, but he kept on coming, swinging the axe blindly as far as I could tell. Snarling and making strange guttural noises that could hardly have been described as human.

He lunged, finally, the axe coming at me again - and I pressed the trigger.

Click! Nothing happened... I was so shocked, I almost failed to step out of the way of the falling axe. What had happened? Had it run out of ammo? No, I'd just seen the guard reload before spraying my window with bullets. Jammed then? Typical... As the axe descended again, I used the rifle like a staff to block it. The head hooked over the body of the gun, so I pulled back this time, wrenching the thing out of Weeks' grasp.

I threw down both weapons with a clatter, stepping away from the man - putting some distance between us and holding out my hand to ward him off. "Look, just stay away... What the fuck is wrong with you?" He simply growled again, gurgling something I couldn't quite catch.

Then he ran at me with a snarl, both hands raised - his intentions obvious. He was going to try and strangle me. I batted his hands aside, bringing my knee up at the same time to double him over. Then I brought down both hands, fingers laced together, onto his back. Weeks fell flat on his face, unmoving.

I bent down and tugged at his belt, freeing it from the loops - then I hogtied him and left him there on the floor. As I was walking away, after picking up the axe and pulling out the pistol, I heard him come to and start his growling once more, but there was no way he was freeing himself from that.

As I turned the corner, I heard a different kind of sound. Not so much growling as grunting... and some groaning. It was coming from one of the rooms off to the right, which the staff used for their tea breaks. I crept slowly towards the sound, and the closer I got the more distinctive it became.

It was the sound of people having sex.

While all that was going on just down the corridor, gunfire and people beating the shit out of each other, someone had decided to have a quickie? They say surviving something like that makes you horny, but still... they didn't even know the gunman had been subdued.

I soon realised my mistake when I peeked round and into that room. These weren't the sounds of a couple having consensual sex at all, but rather those of somebody being raped.

The nurse, whose name I'd never learned, had been shoved back onto the table in the room, while another techie - his white coat hanging off one of his shoulders - worked away. Her clothes were ripped to shreds - blouse, especially - and I saw marks where his nails had raked her flesh. Her skirt had been shoved up around her waist, legs forced apart so he could gain access. She was writhing beneath him, not in ecstasy, but in complete agony - head whipping from side to side, tawny hair all over the place, no longer tied up.

"Hey," I said, jamming the gun into the back of his skull and cocking it loudly so he'd know what it was. "You want to stop that now, you sick bastard."

To my amazement he continued, sped up if anything to reach his climax; to get his own pleasure. The woman looked past him pleadingly at me. Whatever was going on, whatever was making these men do these things, she wasn't affected by it. Well, when I say not affected I mean... Obviously she *was* affected just not— Shit... She hadn't been driven mad, is what I'm trying to get across in my stupid ham-fisted way.

I've never felt more like killing someone in cold blood as I did right then. Never felt more like pulling a trigger and blowing someone away. But I didn't... probably because the memory of that other guy being shot in the head was still too raw. So instead I whacked him on the back of the head with the butt of the pistol. He fell across the nurse, unconscious, and I dragged him off her, let him fall away to the ground. I shook my head as she made to cover herself up again; there were massive welts on her thighs and I wondered how long this had been going on - all the time I'd been trapped behind that glass? "I'm so sorry," I said. I don't know what I was apologising for; not getting there sooner I suppose. Or maybe I was feeling guilty, about the way I had been thinking about her since I got there. For thinking of her as something disposable in my own way, to have a good time with and then bail on.

She said nothing, just continued trying to cover herself up - so I wrenched the man's lab coat off him and handed it to her. "Any... do you have any idea what's...?" I couldn't find the words.

The nurse just shook her head, tears tracking down her cheeks as she pulled the coat around her.

"Come on," I said then. "Let's just get you away from here."

Pause.

CHAPTER TWO

Resume recording:

We made our way down the corridor, but didn't see any more trouble. Just bodies - the guard and Dr Weeks' legacy.

When we reached the lift, and I'd stabbed at the buttons, I found that wasn't working either - again, a consequence of whatever had happened to the electrics maybe? We discovered what that was when we reached the door leading to the staircase; my thinking had been that we could search for anyone else who might be okay, who might be normal - then bundle them into a car and get the fuck out of there.

Looking down the stairwell, we saw smoke - and then flames lapping at one of the lower levels. There was a man standing on the stairs just above it - not running away or trying to get higher, just standing there. He was Hardy to Dr Weeks' Laurel, fat with a moustache. I shouted down to attract his attention, to get him to look up. "Hey... hey mate, move away from there!" The nurse pulled on my arm, perhaps afraid that we were attracting too much attention - or that this guy would turn out to be like the techie back on our floor.

Hardy tilted his head to stare at us, frowning. Then he just started shouting, screaming at the top of his voice. The words were nonsense, a stream of gibberish: "Horse! Potato! Camera! Babies!" His hands were flailing around at the same time, obviously trying to communicate something. Then he started firing off numbers, totally random, no pattern to them at all. "Forty-seven! Hundred and nine! Five, five, *five!!*" There was an exasperation to the last one, frustration at not being able to get his meaning across. It didn't matter in the end, because the flames rose higher - and then the explosion came which made sure that route was blocked off completely.

The fat man was engulfed in the fireball. Didn't stand a chance. The heat even reached us up there, and I pulled the nurse away from the rail to try and shield her. "Shit," I said, glancing down at the devastation beneath us - then looking upwards. Our only way out now was to try for the rooftop, hope there was still a chopper on the landing pad that could get us out of there.

I motioned for us to start our climb and we began going up those stairs, though I could see from the wincing and the way she held the rail that it was painful for the woman beside me. Once or twice she missed her step, and I tried to steady her - but she would flinch and shrug me off. I couldn't blame her for being mistrustful of any man at that point. We'd made it up a couple of flights before it happened: a surge of people came ploughing through a door to our left. At least a dozen, maybe even more - too many to take in all the details, but I could tell that the majority of them weren't right. One man was completely naked, but he'd... done things to his private parts, which were now just a bloodied hole; had castrated himself, and was holding the evidence up high above his head, waving it about. A woman with silver hair, had clawed out her own eyes - she was barking something in Latin. That meant whatever madness had spread throughout this facility wasn't limited to just the men. A third figure had rough slashes across his face as if a bear had clawed him, but then I saw the knife in his hand, the grin he was sporting - and realised he'd also done this to himself.

"Stay b—" I just about managed, but they'd barrelled into us so quickly, taken us completely by surprise. I was shoved back onto the stairs leading upwards, while the group grabbed at the nurse I was with. She punched one guy in the face, but there were simply too many of them. Putting the axe down, I aimed the pistol and fired. It had been a while since I'd been on a range, but you never really forget your target practice lessons - and I'd been pretty good back then. I took down two or three on either side of her, wounding rather than killing, but more poured in from that level - must have been a busy one - grabbing her, and pulling her through. She called out for help as she was dragged inside, and I shot a few more people... before I clicked on empty.

By this time, several had turned their attention to me. I threw the empty gun at one attacker and it bounced off his cheek - didn't even slow him down. So I lifted the axe, hoping the mere sight of it would be enough to put them off. Guess I hadn't really learned anything from those other fights. These fuckers couldn't care less if I had a bazooka.

I turned the axe around, shoved the handle into someone's stomach, before bringing it up and catching him under the chin. Someone else grabbed my arm, swinging me into the wall and sending the axe flying out of my grasp over the rail of the stairway. I ducked the next attack, coming up defensively, crossing my arms to shove the guy back - and it was only then that I realised there were several syringes sticking out of his head at various points; it was one of the most surreal things I'd ever seen. I began fighting my way through the throng, fighting to try and get to the nurse, elbowing people on my left and right. Even before the shots sounded - another smattering of machine-gun fire - I saw the woman being tossed and thrown about beyond the doorway. "Hold on!" I shouted, ignoring more gunfire - but it was already too late. She was torn limb from limb, pulled in every direction until she'd turned into a geyser of red, bathing the crazies in her blood.

Grimacing, I grabbed the nearest person and threw him over the railing to follow that axe, then rammed my rigid fingers into the throat of another, collapsing his windpipe - when the shots rang out near the doorway, bullets spraying the stairs, I beat a hasty retreat. I mean, what else could I do? The tawny-haired nurse was dead; I'd saved her from the maniac who'd been having his way with her, only for the poor woman to suffer an even worse fate. And I still didn't know her name; hadn't thought to ask in all the confusion... That still makes me sad.

I ran up the stairs without looking back - but the crazies weren't interested in following me anyway, even those who weren't being ravaged by whoever was shooting: another guard, or just somebody who'd snatched a gun from one? I made it to the next level, checking the window in the door before walking past it. Fool me once...

It was mayhem on the next few levels we passed, but this was mainly contained on those floors and hadn't reached the stairs yet. By the time I was approaching the top of the building, though, more had appeared and were starting to clamber upwards. They were like ants scaling an ant-hill - so many that I doubted there were any more normals left in the place. But if there wasn't a chopper on the roof when I got there, I'd be screwed. The only option would be to swan dive off the building, which would be quicker than being ripped to shreds or having my privates torn off; the SKIN was tough, but not *that* tough.

Typically, when I reached the door at the top of the building, it was locked shut - another victim of the electrics going down, I figured. Surely backups would have kicked in by now, though; they should have done straight away... But why hadn't the lights been affected? On a different system to the doors, maybe? The sprinklers should also have been activated to douse those fires, I would have thought. None of that was helping me get through that door to the roof.

I leaned over the rail and spotted more and more ants joining in the climb. Bracing myself, I ran at the door and tried to shoulder it open. Didn't budge so much as an inch. I slid down the wall, head in my hands - to have come this far only to fall at the final hurdle... But no, there was always hope. I had to remember that.

No sooner had I thought it than the door opened from the outside. Just popped right open, letting in daylight. A miracle! I scrambled to my feet, ignoring the sound of rampaging footfalls below me, which were getting closer by the second. Turning and nudging the door open more, rushing out through it—

Only to find myself on the wrong end of another Heckler & Koch rifle. Another guard, thickset this time - on the verge of stocky - who'd opened the door and stepped back - was pointing the gun squarely at my chest. The expression on his face was hard to read, and when he cocked his head I figured that would be it. Pulped-noggin time.

"What's... what's going on down there?" he demanded.

I almost cried out with joy - the guy was okay! The look, one of true panic this time. Had probably been up here already when the chaos erupted; hadn't been touched by it yet. "There's... Look, I don't have time to explain," I said to him.

He raised the gun to shoulder level and jabbed at me with it. "Explain now, or I shoot you - right?"

"There are people coming... Something's happened to them; they've gone insane. We need to get out of here before..." I looked past him, searching for a chopper on that rooftop. All this would be irrelevant if there wasn't a way to escape. Yes! A Eurocopter AS355, twin engine - or as we used to more affectionately call them, a twin squirrel. It was one of the most beautiful things I've ever seen. Two seats in the front, four in the back - plenty to get myself and this guy off the roof. "Listen, I can fly that helicopter but we have to go, *right now!*" I said to him.

"You're the one who's insane," he told me. "I'm not going anywhere with—"

"Take a look if you don't believe me," I said, waving a hand for him to step through onto the stairwell and look down. "Only hurry the fuck up."

He skirted around me slowly. "Keep that door open, I'm warning you." The guard backed out, still training the gun on me. He leaned over and cast a glance down the well. I have no idea what he saw, but all the blood had drained from his face when he ran back to me. "Close the fucking door. Close it now!" he ordered.

I waited until he'd stepped clear, then tried to slam the thing shut again. But it wouldn't close. Someone had shoved a fire extinguisher in the gap. I kicked at the metal cylinder, but by that time there were already hands, arms and legs through as well. The extinguisher was gone, but I still couldn't close it - and although I leaned hard against the door, it was obvious there were several people pushing against it from the other side; all desperate to get through and do us as much damage as possible.

The guard had his gun up, aiming at the limbs, but was hesitating. "Do it!" I shouted, having seen what they were capable of - and knowing what wavering might cost us. He swallowed dryly, then fired. The bullets came pretty close to hitting me, but he didn't have a bad aim and a number hit their marks - puncturing arms and legs. Blood spurted from the wounds, but still the people they belonged to wouldn't withdraw. I felt more bodies join these on the other side, and motioned for the guard to come and help me. "I can't hold them on my own!"

He shouldered the rifle and added his bulk to the door, which helped considerably. The noise was incredible: shouting, screaming - even some singing wafting through the gap... an old hymn that rang a bell from my childhood. The man nodded back to the helicopter. "Go... get that thing fired up. I can hold them."

"You sure?"

"Go!" he snapped. What choice did we have - we needed to get the chopper going or it would be overrun before we could take off.

I gave a curt nod and let go of the door, lingering just long enough to make sure it held - or I'd need to lean against it again. Then I sprinted towards the squirrel. As I neared it, I realised that I had no idea whether it had even been left unlocked. Fortunately, the door opened when I tried it - so it was just a matter of starting her up.

I slid into the cockpit, shooting a look across to see how the guard was doing. Not great, it had to be said - the gap widening more and more. A visible thump against it saw him almost lose his footing, but he managed to regain his balance. I didn't have long, though. Quickly, I did pre-flight checks started the engine and got the rotors turning - just in time to witness the guard releasing the door.

The door swung back almost immediately as he started his run towards the chopper, and the first of the crazies piled through. They scrambled over each other, even fought with one another - which bought the man a bit of time - but my God, there were so many... He didn't hesitate to turn and fire, arcing the machine gun and crippling those on the front line. Most had been covered in blood even before he started to shoot; flashes of white from eyes, teeth and what remained of clothing, the only thing breaking up the scene.

He faced me again, made a sprint for it - as I reached around and opened the back door for him, so he could just jump straight in. The thickset man practically ran *into* the helicopter, almost knocking himself out, just like Weeks had done back there with the glass. "Hurry!" I shouted, though I don't think he needed telling. He tossed the rifle inside, and was about to join it when they caught up with him.

All I can remember are the hands, so many hands pulling him back out of the chopper, scratching and punching him; savaging that poor bastard. I made to get out and try to help, but it was already too late for him. I needed to get airborne as quickly as possible. There was a jolt, and I looked back to see that some silly tosser had run headlong into the tail-blade, sending bits of themselves all over the place. That was it; no more. I worked the collective - basically looks like a handbrake - and foot pedals, and we started to rise. The affected were clambering all over the landing skids, weighing us down. I shoved the cyclic - that looks like a joystick - forward, though, and we started to move towards the edge. A few of those crazies fell when we cleared it, but most of them stopped - staring at the chopper from the rooftop, some raising hands as if bidding us a fond farewell.

It was only after I'd been in the air a minute or two that I realised one had climbed into the back through the open door, and was in the well between the rear and front seats. A woman with bald patches in her mousy hair, face burned - like acid had been thrown into it - reached around and grabbed at me. I lost control, the chopper falling towards the ground. I wrestled with my passenger, at the same time trying to wrestle control back of the squirrel. In the end I punched backwards, hoping to hit her - but simultaneously gave a sigh of relief and felt sick to my stomach when I heard the crunching of bone as her nose broke. The grip released, I could fly the chopper upwards once more, but first I shoved the cyclic sideways sharply - causing the woman to fall right out through the back door again. She landed awkwardly, half on grass, half on concrete; her arms and legs creating a Swastika effect.

I levelled out the helicopter, giving a satisfied grunt when the back door slammed shut again, and continued on over the grounds. It was only now I was free of it, that I could see more of the effect of the fire from the outside - some of the windows on the lower levels of the facility had been smashed, letting out thick gouts of smoke. A few of the vehicles in the car park were aflame as well, and now that I was flying towards the fencing, I saw some of those guard dogs tearing into bodies - whether they'd actually killed the men or were just 'playing' with them after the fact was impossible to tell.

One thing I did know, the whole thing was a mess.

I was aware of something sparking off to the side, more gunfire. Someone at the gate was taking pot-shots at the chopper. God almighty, was this ever going to end? I veered off and away, climbing as I did so, hopefully out of range. Leaving the nightmare of that place behind me.

As I flew dead ahead I realised that nobody was going to come to those people's aid, not somewhere as secret as that - not unless I notified the authorities. So, the first thing I did then was get on the radio, trying to hail someone... anyone. I thought I heard a tinny voice answering on one of the frequencies, but after that all I got was static. I kept trying for a little while, all the time moving forwards in a straight line, passing over patchwork countryside and narrow roads below - a chopper was much quicker than driving round all those snaky bends. When the radio went completely dead, I decided to keep going until I found the nearest hint of civilisation and take it from there. I had pretty much a full tank of fuel, according to the gauge; all I had to do was let someone in charge know once I arrived there. Simple, right?

First off, I was much further away from anywhere than I thought - took me a good hour or more to reach the nearest town, and I saw no cottages or houses between the facility and that place I could try. Heaven knows what state the facility would be in by the time I called up the cavalry. It didn't look the largest of towns, but still I offered up a silent "thank you" when I saw buildings: warehouses and shops and fast food places; shielded on the far side by a large river, over which a bridge had been planted.

The closer and lower I flew, though, the more I saw what state the town was in. Smashed storefronts, rubble in the streets. One van was even upside down, either because it had hit something or been flipped - which must have taken several people to do. In short, it looked just as ravaged as the hellhole I'd escaped from. I think I'd assumed that whatever had happened at the facility had been contained to that place alone; it never entered my head that this might be a more widespread thing; that it might have happened anywhere else at the same time.

Yet I saw evidence of the same thing here - dead bodies everywhere. Live ones too, only they were running around, acting in that lunatic way I was familiar with. People beating each other with fists and rocks, mutilating each other with teeth and blades; others had stripped naked, fucking out in the open - not just couples, but dozens of them in scenes that would have made Caligula blush.

I couldn't stop here. I wouldn't find the civilisation I was looking for here. Only death and depravity, a new Sodom and Gomorrah. I'd already decided to move on to the next town or city when the chopper gave another lurch. Wasn't anyone inside this time, no crazies in the back seat - nobody shooting at me, either. No, this was something happening internally. Something engine-related. The rotors above me began to slow down, the nose dipping as we fell; an alarm sounded, loud and annoying. I was right over the town, over the danger zone - I couldn't drop here... Couldn't, and yet I *was*; it was out of my control.

The chopper began to spin, then to roll... Over and over. I'd forgotten to strap myself in, hadn't had time when I first got behind the controls and had been too busy with other things afterwards, so I rolled with the machine - hitting the roof, being smashed against the floor. The collective struck my side and I cried out in pain.

At some point the rotors just broke off, and the tail hit the side of a building, but that's pretty much all I remember before I blacked out.

Before I thought I'd died.

Stop. Playback.

CHAPTER THREE

Record:

Wow - that was a lot to bombard you with, wasn't it?

Took a while to play that all back - it's almost dark now - and thought to myself *not bad, Adam*. I think I more or less captured what a shitstorm that escape from the facility was, then the crash. I hope I did anyway, hard to tell. Nobody to play this out loud to here, but me.

Dramatic wasn't it? Tense? Got the blood pumping? Yeah? That's great...

Pause.

Resume record:

More or less ready to continue, though it's been hard gearing myself up to carry on. I might joke about it...you could tell I was joking, right? About how dramatic it all was. But actually, reliving all that... I shivered at one point. I never shiver. Never get cold, the SKIN sees to that. Regulates body temp. And looking back, listening to all that again, I know how lucky I am. What a million to one shot it was I'd be wearing the SKIN in the first place when...

You want to know what happened, don't you? After the crash. Here I am babbling about my feelings, back then and when I heard my story again - but I left it on what they might call a cliffhanger in those old serials I used to watch as a kid on Saturday morning TV. Well, not that much of a cliffhanger because you know I made it, I didn't die. Haven't yet anyway. But here's why I didn't back then.

When I woke up, it was still black... quite dark, at any rate. In fact, I had a little trouble realising I *was* awake to begin with. I blinked a few times, brought my hand up to a sore spot on my head. Should have come away wet, by rights, but the SKIN had contained the wound underneath, was already recycling my spilled blood, speeding up the healing process. Nothing's ever wasted.

I heard movement off to my left and made to get up, remembering where I'd crashed - what had happened at the facility, what had been happening below me in the town. If I was still alive, I wouldn't stay that way if the affected had found me. I let out a moan at the pain in my side where the collective had banged into me, but fortunately hadn't torn the SKIN.

"Don't move!" said a voice; male. "I'm warning you!"

If he was speaking to me, and not trying to either kill me or shag me, then I figured I was okay. Slowly, I turned to look in his direction - and I saw the guard's gun, the one that had been in the back of the chopper, pointing at me for the second time. It was in the hands of a guy of about fifty - with bushy eyebrows and a beard to match - wearing a white shirt with the sleeves rolled up, and light grey trousers. I raised both my hands in surrender. "There's no need for that. I'm okay."

He looked at me sideways on, with suspicion. The light in the room flickered and it was then I realised it was coming from some candles. One quite close, a few more back there in the gloom, like they were deliberately keeping it dim.

"Where... where am I? How did I get—"

The man's eyebrow's met in the middle, and his grip on the rifle tightened. "I'll be the one asking the questions."

"Fair enough," I said.

"Who are you?" was the first one.

"My name is Adam Keller."

"Where are you from?"

"What originally? Well, my mother was from—"

"Don't get bloody smart with me."

"I wasn't."

It went on in that same vein for a little while until we got to the meat of it. I told him that I'd come from a hospital - thought that would be better than a heavily guarded R&D facility - about an hour away, but not to ask me where, because I didn't even know where *this* place was.

"Hospital? Don't know of any hospitals that far out, just our local one," he said. I was trying to get a handle on his accent, not that it would tell me anything - he might have moved to this town for all I knew. Northern was about as close as I got.

"Well, you asked me..."

"That why you're dressed like that?" he used the barrel of the rifle to point to my shorts.

"Er... yeah, that's right."

"Where'd you get the gun?"

"What?"

"*This* gun." He shook it for emphasis. "The one we found in the wreck with you." Now we were starting to get somewhere. *We*... so he wasn't alone, and I had him to thank for dragging me out of the crashed chopper before any of the affected could get to me. "Military hospital, was it? You some kind of soldier?"

"Some... something like that," I replied.

"Ask him about that stuff. What's wrong with his skin?" Another voice - female - came from the back of the room.

"Who—" I began and promptly got cut off.

"Answer her," said the man. "What's wrong with you,

why're you scaly like that?"

From a distance, they might not have noticed - but up close, dragging me back here, they couldn't fail to clock the SKIN. "It's... kind of hard to explain," I said.

He looked at me, puzzled. I wasn't sure myself what exactly this thing was, so I sure as hell couldn't explain it to this guy; he needed Weeks, and I'd left him hog-tied and barking in that corridor. "There something wrong with you? That it? That why you were in the hospital?"

"Yeah... that's right."

"It's not... you know, contagious is it?" This was the woman again.

"No," I promised her, shaking my head. "No, it's not."

"That why you're bald, too?" The man again.

"Listen, doesn't matter. What matters is that most of the people back there where I was being... treated just went nuts, same as they did here. Something's happened and—"

"Something's fucking happened, all right!"

"Dennis!" The woman scolded. "You're scaring Jane."

Now I knew there were at least three of them.

"She *should* be bloody well scared," said the man, but his tone had already softened.

"If he's with the military, maybe he knows what's going on," the woman said. And then, suddenly, she moved closer to one of the candles. She was slightly younger than the man, her hair shoulder length. It was hard to tell in that light, because everything had an orange glow, but it looked a reddish colour - probably from a bottle. She was holding someone's hand: a little girl, presumably Jane, who was wearing a school uniform - black jumper and trousers, white shirt, and clutching a backpack. The pig-tails completed the look of innocence.

I shook my head again. "Sorry lady, but I have to confess that I don't have the first clue what's happening - or why."

"Carrie," the woman said then. "My name is Carrie McCall."

"Pleased to meet you, Carrie. You too, Jane." I nodded at the girl, then the man. "Even you, Dennis. I think I have you guys to thank for saving me."

"We were looking for more folk like us," said another voice now, and a young man in his late teens or early twenties with a much darker complexion stepped forward. He was wearing jeans and a hoodie, his hair close-cropped. "Found you instead. I'm Rakesh."

"Well, I'm very grateful. And hi Rakesh." These people were survivors, like me. Maybe the only people in this godforsaken town who were normal - and they'd been doing the same thing that I was trying to do back at the facility, gather together anyone who wasn't with the affected. Band together to protect each other, to live. To give each other hope.

"Dennis, will you put that thing down before you hurt someone," said Carrie, and the man finally lowered the rifle... a little. "It's obvious Adam's not like—" She paused, unwilling or unable to say any more.

"I'm not," I replied, filling in. "I'm *really* not. Can I just ask, how long has it been since you dragged me out and brought me here?"

"A good few hours," Rakesh told me. "Maybe half a day." So, definitely night-time out there; maybe even almost dawn.

"And where exactly *is* here?"

"The White Hart," said Dennis, with more than a hint of pride in his voice. "Miccleston. My pub."

Didn't look like any kind of pub I'd ever drank in, or

even got drunk in. But then the more my eyes adjusted, the more light was thrown out by those candles and the more of my surroundings I could make out. Barrels, shelving with bottles on them, boxes of crisps. "We're in a cellar," I said.

"Give that man a cigar," sniped Dennis, pulling up an empty crate and sitting down hard on it; so hard it almost collapsed underneath him.

Not a bad place to hole up. There were provisions at least - and enough booze to make sure you didn't care that the end of the world was apparently here. No, I told myself, there's nothing to say it's happened *anywhere* else. Just the two places so far that have torn themselves to pieces.

"And you all know each other?"

"We do now," answered Rakesh.

"Any of you together?" I was thinking Dennis and Carrie surely - they spoke to each other like an old married couple - but apparently not. They lived on opposite sides of town, complete strangers until... I nodded then at her and Jane, thinking they might be mother and daughter; some kind of blood link between them that might explain the immunity.

"I'm... I live not far from her school; I know her mum and dad a little." Carrie turned to Jane, said: "Sweetie, why don't you go and do some more of that colouring in? Over there, right next to that candle where the light's better." The girl looked at her, then nodded, fishing stuff out of her backpack before heading off across the cellar. Carrie lowered her voice. "When it... The kids were just coming out of school when it happened. I can see them from my window, always makes me smile; they're so full of energy. Takes me back." She had a faraway look in her eye, as if she was remembering her own childhood days. "It's always quite lively, boisterous. Only something was off this time, something not right. The kids were fighting, but then that's nothing new - only it was the *way* they were fighting with each other. It was just more..."

"Savage?" I offered.

Carrie gave a nod. "They were really laying into each other, doing some damage. Not just to each other, to themselves as well. One lad was simply standing there punching himself in the face. But it wasn't just the kids, it was the teachers too - and parents. I watched for a few moments, not really knowing what to do... I got up off the sofa finally when I saw all the blood; when there were kids on the ground not moving. I tried to call the police, but the line was dead. So I got my shoes and coat on, went outside - just in time to see Jane running towards me, terrified. Her mother was chasing her, but she wasn't trying to get her back, to keep her safe. Sandra had this odd expression on her face, a wild look in her eye, you know?"

I did. I knew exactly what she meant.

"Jane basically leapt into my arms. I think she had a sense that her mother wanted to do something to her as well. I took her back into my house, just as Sandra caught up. She was banging on that door, trying to get in - but she wasn't shouting anything, just wailing. Screaming and wailing. I held Jane to me in the hallway; she was sobbing into my shoulder. Then the banging suddenly stopped. I don't know what happened to Sandra, whether she just gave up or someone..." Carrie looked back across at Jane, busily colouring something in, tongue sticking out of the corner of her mouth.

"What did you do then?" I asked.

"I waited a little while, but the noise was deafening outside - like a full scale riot or something. When someone put the living room window through, I took Jane out the back door, out into the garden, and we climbed over the fence. Wasn't until then, until we were making our way through town, that I saw it had affected more than just the school."

I recalled the images I'd seen as I flew over the place. There was no need for Carrie to go into any more detail.

"I just couldn't get my head around it. How quickly it had turned... for everything to go to rack and ruin, to go to rot. If Rakesh hadn't found us, I don't know what would have happened." She looked across at the youth and smiled a thank you.

"So," I said next, "what's your story, Rakesh?"

Turned out he was a student at the local college. "Moved here to study art," the lad told me. "Painting, drawing, film..."

"Piss about at the tax payer's expense more like," Dennis chipped in, but Rakesh didn't rise to the bait.

He'd been walking back to his digs after a lecture on Picasso, taking a short-cut down an alleyway leading into town proper, when he became aware of someone following him. "There was a gang of them; guys, about my age. It's not the first time something like that's happened," he said with a sigh in his voice. "Things can get a bit difficult... especially up here." I thought I noticed a pointed exchange of glances between him and Dennis, but he moved on quickly. "It's like Carrie said, though, there was just something off about them. The way they were moving, the funny noises they were making. Wasn't right. So I ran, raced up the alley - and they chased me. Managed to lose them eventually, but I was scared they'd still be waiting to jump me somewhere. You can imagine how relieved I was when I spotted a copper on patrol. I'd been about to phone for help, when I saw him - went up to him. Except..."

"What?" I prompted.

"Well, when he turned and looked at me... his face was blank. It was as if there was nothing going on inside, like he was just reacting to the tap on the shoulder automatically. Nobody at home, you know..." Rakesh pointed to his temple, "...up here. He was drooling; reminded me of Nan that time when she had the stroke, and... I could smell something. As if he'd messed himself or whatever. When I looked down, the front of his trousers were wet as well. His eyes were going in different directions; he was in a proper bad way. I was going to call for an ambulance, but that's when the gang caught up with me, all grunting and snarling. I braced myself for what they were about to do, but it was the policeman they went for first. Some part of them must have remembered that they hated the police more than..." He hung his head and shook it. "I ran off. Wanted to stay and help him, but there were just too many of them - and I'm not much of a fighter. Never have been. Used to get bullied all the time at school, but could never dish it back out."

"That's not a bad thing," I told him, at the same time thinking that perhaps it was, given this new situation. That if you didn't fight, you would never survive it.

As if reading my mind, Rakesh said: "It might be. I think I'm going to have to learn; the things I saw out there... Before I ran into Carrie and Jane."

"You mentioned your phone - did you try to use it after the thing with the cop?"

"Reception's rubbish at the best of times out here, but it's completely dead at the moment - at least on mine. No net, no service; nothing."

Okay, that was my radio, the landline Carrie had said was out, and now Rakesh's mobile. "So," I said, trying to change the subject, "you all ended up here, in the cellar of a pub?"

"Dennis spotted us wandering down the street, ushered us down through the cellar doorway."

"Just in time too, there was a car weaving its way towards them. Out of control it was. I could see what was going to happen as plain as day," Dennis informed us. "It ended up smacking into the post office opposite."

"But how did you come to be down here in the first place?" I asked him.

"What kind of stupid question is that?"

I shrugged.

"It was the safest bleedin' place to go when all the shit hit the fan. I can lock the door to the cellar from the inside, and there's a way out through the cellar doors I saw them through." Dennis thumbed back at Carrie and Rakesh. "I've seen this place turn ugly before, usually after a match night - or on Friday or Saturday when it comes to chucking out time - but this was something else. And in the middle of the fucking day! No warning, nothing. Weren't even that many people in here; dozen or more. Started when Franny, that's my...was my barmaid." He paused, composing himself. "She was serving this customer - well-to-do kinda bloke. Smart suit, wanted one of those poncy lagers that they think makes 'em look so cool. Franny was pulling that for him, chatting away like always - nothing flirty, she wasn't that kind of girl. Definitely nothing that should have provoked what happened next, when he just reached across the bar and grabbed her... you know... *grabbed* her." Taking one hand off the rifle, now resting across his knees, Dennis made a squeezing gesture to illustrate what had happened. "Just out of the blue, right there in front of everyone. Molesting her. 'Course, Franny slaps him, as you would - but that doesn't stop this guy. He's holding on for dear life, squeezing harder, hurting her."

It was the kind of behaviour I'd come to associate with some of the affected, reduced virtually to animals - acting on their basest instincts, whether that was to kill or to mate.

"I was over there quicker than you can say Jack Robinson, obviously. He ignored my warnings to let go of her, so I just smacked him straight in the jaw." Here was someone who was the exact opposite of Rakesh, no stranger to a brawl or several. Probably grew up learning how to use his fists; definitely a plus when it came to running a pub I would have imagined. "Still he didn't let go, even when I grabbed his collar and pulled him in - gave him a couple more taps. His face was a right old fucking mess by this time, but he didn't seem to care. Then the other crap started, the two lads at the pool table knocking seven bells out of each other with the cues - and when one of those snapped, the guy began stabbing his mate with the broken end. Like he was Peter Cushing fighting Christopher Lee. A couple of the older regulars - retired, wouldn't hurt a fly - they were throwing darts at each other, until one pulled the board off the wall and hit his friend with it. So there I was, in the middle of all that, rushing from one disaster to another, trying to calm things down and thinking *just what the hell is going on?* When I look over and see that the fellow in the suit is still at it, only he's pulled Franny over the bar now and is—" He looked around the make sure Jane was still occupied by the colouring book; she was. "You know, doing things to himself over her. Had his trousers down and was... doing things."

Look, I'm sorry - again this isn't probably something you want to hear. But I figure it's best to lay it all out, document it. Didn't happen to me, but I'm relating it as faithfully as I can, what I can remember about that conversation. Might not be the exact words, but you get the gist... sadly.

"Then before he's done, another customer has gone behind the bar, got a bottle of vodka and is standing on the counter pouring the spirits onto them. Before I could do anything about it, he's got a lighter out and he's chucked it down onto them." Dennis used his free hand to wipe his face. "I mean, I've never seen anything like that before in my life. Franny was screaming at the top of her lungs, but the bloke with the trousers round his ankles - well, shit, he was laughing as he burned to death. Laughing! I mean, for fuck's sake! Like he wasn't wired up right. By the time I got to them, so I could use the extinguisher on them, it was already too late."

Wasn't long after that, and certainly not long after Dennis had seen what was happening out on the street beyond the pub, that he retreated to the safest place he could think of.

"I heard the ones that were left in the pub go outside, join the rest of those freaks out there. There's a gap in the cellar door, the one that leads to the street, and I watched them all going on their rampage – before finally heading off somewhere else. I tried the lights, but there was no power on at all, so I lit these candles. It was about an hour later, maybe two, when I spotted those three in trouble out there, so I got them to safety."

"But if you four are okay, it proves that not everyone went mad. Not everyone was affected."

"Right," Rakesh answered. "Which was why we went out to try and find some others."

"Pretty brave thing to do," I told him, remembering what he'd said about not being a fighter.

He shrugged. "I'd been found. Figured I needed to pay that forward."

"Me and him were out there looking around when we heard your crash," Dennis chipped in. "When we found you. Got you out, and carried you the couple of streets back here."

"You're lucky to be alive, Adam." That was Carrie; she had absolutely no idea.

It was at this point, after they'd all got their stories off their chests, that they asked me to fill them in on what exactly had happened to me. Only fair, I suppose, so I gave them the edited highlights. Techies and guards became doctors and security men, escaping from my level became an escape from the ward... I didn't have to change what had happened to that nurse though, and I could see Carrie pulling a face as I went through it with them.

When Dennis started asking too many questions again, about my 'condition', about the military angle and rifle, I deflected it by asking: "So, what do we think's happened here? Any ideas?"

"Some kind of mass hysteria?" offered Carrie, biting her bottom lip.

"Mass panic, you mean? Something usually sets that off though, doesn't it?" I said.

"Like when that radio programme convinced everyone there was an alien invasion. People are sheep," spat Dennis. "Especially his generation."

Rakesh was still doing very well to bite his tongue.

"No, I don't think it was that," I said to steer the conversation in another direction again. "Too spontaneous, too random. More like a plague."

"Wasn't there some sort of dancing plague in the middle ages?" said Carrie.

"I think you're right... My dad was into history," I added by way of an explanation.

"Didn't a lot of the people involved die from heart attacks or whatever, simply because they couldn't stop dancing? There were hundreds of them, if I remember rightly," Carrie continued.

"My ex-missus used to read horror books," said Dennis. "Tried them once, but wasn't a big fan. I do remember a couple by this guy though - one was about the earth heating up and mass hallucinations, people seeing these weird grey figures. Another one was where adults suddenly turned on teenagers and kids, tried to kill them all. It was in the blood..." Dennis realised that everyone was looking at him, then said: "Personally, I reckon it was some kind of chemical weapon. One of his lot." He jabbed at finger in Rakesh's direction and that was it; the lad was shoving himself off the wall, heading towards Dennis.

For his part the publican was rising, bringing the gun around.

"Whoa, whoa!" I said, standing now and getting

between them. "You really want to do this? Don't you think we've got enough problems, without turning on each other?"

"You, soldier, soldier," Dennis said, training the weapon in my direction. "Sit the fuck down."

"*All* of you sit down," said Carrie, nodding over towards Jane, who had her head down over her colouring book, arms covering herself up - body wracking with each sob as she cried her little heart out. She went over, bending and putting her own arms around the child, who turned and flung herself into Carrie - just as she had done when her mother had tried to kill her. Jesus, what that might do to a child... Kid was probably still in some kind of shock.

"She's right," I said. "This isn't helping."

Rakesh walked away, back into the shadows of the cellar where he'd been when I first woke up. Dennis glared at me, waiting for me to do as he'd ordered - sit down again. When I backed off, holding my hands up, and sat down on the floor again, he took his seat on the crate once more, watching me. Studying me, just like those scientists had done back at the facility.

And for some reason, I felt like I was... that *all of us* were in more danger from him and his wild temper than any number of the affected.

Stop.

CHAPTER FOUR

Record:

Sorry for the break, felt like a good place to stop and move on a little before continuing. I need to keep moving, keep trudging on. But I know I also need to continue with the story, get you up to speed before making any future recordings.

I listened to the last instalment before dropping off to sleep last night, just to get it clear in my mind where I'd left things. So, we were in that pub cellar - and for a while it kind of worked. I say a while, it was probably only a few days that we played "happy" families down there. The atmosphere was always tense, but then it would be with Dennis the way he was. My head and my side healed quite nicely though, thanks to the SKIN. There was food and bottled water, so the four of them were okay - except I didn't, *couldn't* really have any. And I think I'd started to figure out that whatever was causing this might be in the air - that I might not be like Dennis, Carrie, Rakesh and Jane. That I might not be immune to its effects, and if I simply took the SKIN off and started noshing on dry roasted peanuts, I could become like one of the affected in seconds. Might end up throttling someone. Maybe even Dennis... I might even have enjoyed that.

No. Bad joke. Definitely, considering how—

Backtracking, don't worry. Carrie was really the only one who noticed I wasn't eating or drinking, kept telling me, "You need to keep your strength up, someone in your condition." She still thought I was sick; ironic really.

"No, honestly. I'm good."

In the end I took the proffered packets of crisps, the

bottles of water, and I'd pretend to eat them - just out of sight, when the others weren't looking. I'd do the same with going to the loo, which we all did privately in the far corner of the cellar anyway. I'd imagine the stink was terrible by then - I was thankful the SKIN filtered it out.

There were no more scouting missions, mainly because I don't think Rakesh and Dennis wanted to go out there with each other anymore - and partly because Dennis didn't want to leave me unguarded; he even slept with that gun across his lap, probably made him feel better. They could have gone out separately, but then that would have meant Dennis trusting Rakesh with the rifle out there - and in all honesty, I still don't think he would have lasted ten minutes alone - or trusting him to watch me down in the cellar. He wasn't about to give the weapon to Carrie, either, because she'd already made up her mind I wasn't a threat. Besides, if there were pockets of survivors out there, the crazies definitely outweighed them, and if they hadn't gone to ground somewhere they'd probably be dead. They'd be just as hard to find now as we would be.

So we trod water. I think some part of them all wanted to stay there, though, and pretend none of what had happened had really happened. Maybe wait for rescuers who didn't even know we were there. Stranded on our own distant planet...

"At some point we're going to have to go out there again, you know," I argued once or twice. "We can't just sit around here forever." That would be worse than being trapped behind that glass, trapped in the facility. I couldn't even get Carrie's support on that one; not even when we heard people above us in the pub itself, noise and general mayhem - and we'd had to stay quiet, Carrie telling Jane it was all just a game, like the one her mother had been playing with her. That soon they'd see each other again and Jane's mum would be back to her old self.

It couldn't go on, however, and the tipping point came during yet another argument. Dennis had been going on about the chemical weapons thing again - another reason I was glad I hadn't told the truth about where I'd come from - ranting about terrorism and all that bullshit, as if Rakesh had anything to do with any of that. As if it even mattered anymore after the past week.

Rakesh had been brave enough to go for the gun this time, to try and take it from Dennis - and they'd wrestled with it. I thought at one point the thing was going to go off. Carrie had been shouting about upsetting Jane again, had gone over to where the girl had been working on yet another project the woman had come up with to keep her occupied - cutting out shapes she'd coloured in, making patterns which she'd eventually show to the art expert Rakesh, who'd nod approvingly whatever they looked like.

Jane had covered up her head again, as she did whenever these kinds of rows kicked off, so Carrie went over and rubbed her shoulders - trying to calm her down, to calm the sobs that were beginning. I didn't see what happened next, though, because I was concentrating on what was happening with Dennis and Rakesh. But I saw the aftermath, when the screaming started.

By the time I glanced over again, Carrie was staggering backwards. She looked like she was crying as well, hands up to her face. It was only when she took these down that I saw the wounds there, the ragged holes in her cheeks. Carrie's screams were shrill, causing *all* of us to pause and look over. Jane was rising from her work, a pair of scissors still fixed in her hand which were dripping blood. The girl was crying all right, but from laughter rather than sadness. And before any of us could do a thing to stop her, she'd leapt up to carry on stabbing Carrie - this time in the neck and chest. The woman did her best to ward her off, arms flailing around, but in the end it was no use. She toppled backwards, into a shelf that had bottles on it - knocking everything flying. The screaming was replaced by smashing glass as Carrie slumped down to the ground, not moving.

Rakesh let go of the gun, let Dennis take it - maybe

realising that whoever had it would be forced to make a really tough decision. We'd all seen people who had become affected, knew what they looked like, how they acted; for whatever reason, Jane had been slow to display the symptoms and we'd all just assumed she was immune. There was no way of knowing, no doctors to test her, to analyse her for... whatever the hell this was. When it had struck, it hit so many people at once; if you didn't turn then it was safe to assume you were okay... or so we'd - I'd - thought. It was an assumption that had cost Carrie her life.

When Jane ran across the room, she ran quickly - and with the energy of youth, powered seemingly by the transformation that was overtaking her. "Dennis..." I said; which was all I thought needed saying. He was the one with the gun, the one she was targeting. Dennis levelled it at her, grinding his teeth. I could see his finger twitching on the trigger. A few seconds ago he'd been fighting with Rakesh over the possession of that firearm - who knows, might have even shot the lad if it had continued. But now he was reluctant to use it when he really needed to; not that I could blame him, not that I'd have done any different. Jane was affected, but she was still a child. One who, up until only a few moments ago, had been colouring in, making pictures, doing the normal things that kids do. Now she was a stone cold killer, with one notch already on her belt - and a second imminent.

Dennis did at least attempt to fend her off, dropping the rifle - maybe in the hopes that someone else would pick it up and do what he'd been unable to - then grabbing her by the shoulders. "Jane... Jane, *please!*" In all my time in that cellar, I'd never heard Dennis so vulnerable, so unsure of what to do. Jane was snarling at him, teeth chomping together like she wanted to eat him - though I'd never seen any of the affected showing signs of cannibalism. Then she ducked out of his grasp, twisting and turning and sliding underneath. Whether it was pure "luck" or by design, she stabbed him on the inside of the leg - and must have hit an artery. His trousers turned dark quickly, exactly how I imagine the policeman's had when Rakesh went to him for help. Dennis' teeth were clamped together now, his hand going to the wound – but Jane was already stabbing him again.

Rakesh had been backing away even before Jane set off, so I reached down for the rifle. I hadn't been thinking about more than just grabbing it, more than taking charge, but once I had it I was the one facing that tough decision about Jane. In the end it was taken out of my hands because she headed off in the other direction after the teenager, springing up and onto him, scissors going to work on him too. I raised the rifle, but then the pair of them – a weird amalgamation of bodies, a flurry of arms and hands – stumbled sideways into a crate that had a candle on it. Not something that would have mattered ordinarily, if it hadn't been for all those spirits Carrie had already spilled.

There were whooshing sounds, and suddenly a wall of flames sprang up – cutting me off from them. I looked over towards Dennis, but he was on the floor as well, swimming in a pool of his own blood. I thought about a tourniquet, but he'd already lost so much... and where would I take him, even if I got him out? Wasn't like I could pop him round to the nearest A&E department, get them to stitch him up and pump some plasma into him. The twitching stopped at that point anyway, the last throes of death done with. I didn't – and still don't really – know who was better off, me or him. Me or Carrie, or Rakesh.

The fire continued to spread, running along with the river of spirits and setting light to any wood it could find, eating it up like a greedy mongrel after scraps. Cutting off my way to the cellar doors, to the street, and leaving only one exit route. Up and out through the door that led to the pub, the one Dennis had used to escape the chaos up there in the first place. I stepped over the body, tried not to look at the others that were being consumed by flames. That cellar was like what had happened in miniature – how everything had been okay one minute, then turned to shit the next. And once again I was climbing to get away from an all-consuming fire.

I was about halfway up the steps, looking over my shoulder, when a figure flew at me out of those flames. Too small to be Rakesh, it had to be Jane - the girl a human torch, clothes burning up on her. But she showed no signs of being in pain, just driven to attack; the same drive that had started all this in the first place. Remarkably, she also still had the scissors in her grasp, ready to do more damage. With her free hand, though, she caught my calf - pitching me onto the stairs. Jane brought down the scissors, and if I hadn't rolled over to face her they would have gone straight into me - SKIN or no SKIN. As it was, the blades got stuck in the wood of the steps, giving me time to kick out, and knock her back. Oddly, her current state made it easier to fight her - she was looking less and less like the girl Carrie had cared for. Less and less *human* as I struggled to scramble away. That said, I still couldn't bring myself to shoot her - so instead I struck her at the temple with the butt of the rifle and watched her tumble down the steps, rolling and rolling to meet the fire once more.

I flipped back over, half-crawling and half-stumbling up towards the door. Luckily, Dennis had left the key in the lock, so I turned it and practically fell out through the doorway into the pub, slamming the door behind me and locking it again from that side. I tossed away the key and leant against the door.

There was a bang from the other side that made me jump, but it wasn't enough to break down the barrier - Jane didn't have the strength for that. I couldn't just stand there and listen as the thumps grew weaker and weaker, though; I needed to be away from that place. Be on my way somewhere... anywhere. The whole pub would go up eventually anyway.

I hadn't even thought about whether there might still be any of the affected upstairs. It had been a little while since we'd heard anyone up there, but that didn't mean a thing; they could have just been standing, staring into space for all I knew. Thankfully, it was completely deserted - just the dead that had met their end in the initial event Dennis had described, including the charred remains of the barmaid and the guy in the suit, the foam from the fire extinguisher having hardened over them here and there. It seemed pretty pointless now, not just because they'd been dead or dying when Dennis did it, but because fire would still claim this whole building soon.

As I picked my way through the bar area, I did my best to ignore the other sights, keeping the Heckler & Koch up and ready for any trouble. I reached the window and saw that it was still daylight outside; I'd sort of lost track of the time, of the days down there, because it was always dark apart from the candles and the narrow slit of light that seeped through the doors to the street. Smoke was already reaching me from the cellar so it was time to get out. A quick check of the street revealed that it was just as quiet out there; no sign of anyone at all. Of course, the affected could pop up out of nowhere at a moment's notice, as I'd seen, but I had the gun and was willing to risk it.

Not looking back, I headed out through the main door of the pub. Moving forward, always moving forward.

Pause.

Resume recording:

I spent the next couple of hours making my way through those streets, which were uncannily quiet. *Perhaps all the affected had wiped themselves out*, I thought to myself. But then where were the bodies, if that was the case? Not that there weren't a fair few of those, don't get me wrong.

Wasn't long after leaving *The White Hart*, though, that I came across somewhere I could grab some clothes. My time with Dennis and co. had made me realise that I needed to blend in more, cover the SKIN to avoid any questions I couldn't really answer. The shop was an old Army & Navy store – just the one arm of the forces missing, which happened to be mine, naturally. It had been broken into already, or at least the glass at the front had been smashed.

Taking a leaf out of Rakesh's book, I swiped a dark hoodie from a rack and tugged that on, then I pulled the hood up and over a baseball cap. A pair of cargos fitted over my shorts, and of course I had my boots already, courtesy of the facility. I found a grey overcoat to complete the outfit, which would also hide the rifle quite nicely, then I tugged a pair of gloves over the SKIN on my hands. Finally, I filled a backpack with things I thought might be useful, like a compass; a few maps; binoculars; that kind of thing. A backpack, which was just a little bigger than Jane's school one had been...

Jane.

I tried to push away thoughts of what had happened to that little girl, but it wasn't easy. If there'd been a delay in her turning, then why not with others? Could anyone now be trusted? Was anyone actually immune to this thing? Made me all the more grateful for the SKIN; I was starting to realise that it was the only thing keeping me safe... that would continue to do so, with a bit of luck.

Being in that store was the first time since it had all happened I'd been able to catch my - recycled - breath, and thinking about Jane brought back memories not just of Carrie, Rakesh and Dennis, but of the people back at the facility. The kindly doctor Weeks, that nurse, the guard on the roof; all victims of this in their different ways; and even the affected were still people deep down. Maybe they could even be cured, a reversal set in motion. It would take greater minds than mine to figure all that out, but it did start me thinking; it gave me a direction and maybe some shreds of optimism.

For most of the rest of that day, I checked out some of the other buildings in town - clearing rooms before searching them for anything useful; seeing if any phone lines were working, whether there were any mobile signals. In only one of those houses was electricity still powering the lights, but I couldn't get either the desktop computer or the laptop working. I tell a lie, the laptop did power up for about a minute, enough to show me what looked like a scrambled screensaver of clouds. Oh God, what I wouldn't have given for a plane at that point; to be soaring through the clouds, up and away from all that shit on the ground. Then the thing just died on me, and it wasn't long after that the lights winked out as well.

There was just no consistency to it. If the power was out, then it should have been out everywhere - not randomly. And why didn't it last? When it grew dark, I didn't want to be out on the streets alone - there was a night vision scope on the rifle, which helped, but that wasn't the point. I wasn't ready back then. So I found another hiding place till dawn: an out of the way garage I could bed down in, surrounded by cardboard boxes, which I could easily defend or get out of if it was attacked. I'd already decided that, come the morning, I would find a car and get out of there, give myself some time to think.

I hadn't slept much during my time in that cellar, napping more than anything - and I doubted I would that night either. If I'm on edge, I always have trouble nodding off and even then I sleep incredibly lightly - which works well if you have one ear out for any potential trouble. But I found myself dozing, through sheer exhaustion I suspect, and my dreams were filled with beautiful countryside similar to the kind I'd flown over in the chopper.

I was snapped out of that by the cardboard boxes falling over. Someone in the garage with me. Immediately, I swung the rifle round in that direction... letting out the breath I was holding when I saw it was just a cat. A tabby, it jumped down from the boxes it had knocked off, and padded towards me on the floor.

"Hey there," I said. "You're not going to make me use this, are you?"

It stood and gazed at me, cocking its head. For a moment or two I wasn't quite sure whether it would go for me or not, but then it started cleaning itself - licking its paws and rubbing its ears with them. Unaffected by everything that had been going on around it the past few days, unaffected by whatever had touched the population.

Then it was on its way, off to continue its nocturnal activities now that it had woken me up. I waited there until dawn's early light started to stream in through the small window, only then emerging from my hiding place behind the boxes, my hiding place inside the garage - though not before selecting a few choice items that were on the walls: tools that I could use as hand-to-hand weapons should the need arise - a smaller brother to the axe from back at the facility, a hammer, a small serrated saw that tucked into itself like a pocket knife.

There was still no activity out on the streets, and I headed - according to my compass - out towards the northern-most end of town. I came across a few cars, and one truck, but couldn't seem to get any of them started. Probably just as well, because the noise would have attracted too much attention before I could leave the place behind me in my rear-view. Much better, I reasoned, to take one from the edge of town and quickly say my goodbyes. Keep quiet until then, stick to the spaces between buildings which would hide me. Assuming I could find a car that was actually working, of course.

Eventually I did: a red Ford parked up not far away from the local theatre. Abandoned, like most of them - I wondered if the affected could remember *how* to drive anymore, or even wanted to - with its keys still in the ignition. It started up first time and purred more contently than the tabby had done back in that garage. I'd make a clean getaway; hadn't seen any of the crazies in all this time, let alone had to fight any of them. But I was really counting my chickens...

I didn't know where they'd been, or where they came from - but suddenly there were dozens of them; the streets choking with them and their noise. It was almost as if they'd decided to let me get this far, give me the hope that I might make it away from town, only to snatch that away from me at the last minute. Out of the buildings all around me they streamed, like someone had rung a dinner bell, or issued a call to arms. Too many to shoot, that was for sure. The only way was to get in the Ford and drive.

So that's what I did, getting ahead of them for a little while - only to find more in front of me. I couldn't really avoid them, had to plough into men, women and children. Wasn't even sure whether they were all affected or not, and couldn't stop to find out. I just prayed I was ending their suffering as they bounced over the bonnet, over the roof. It was then that I felt a rumbling beneath me, the car vibrating, followed by what sounded like an explosion going off. The next thing I knew, a crater the size of a small pond had appeared in front of me; a massive hole in the road! Was that what they were doing, had they set some sort of trap for me, like natives in a jungle? They'd never shown any kind of aptitude for working together before - in fact quite the reverse - but...

I tugged on the steering wheel to swerve round the hole, sideswiping more of the affected as I did so. One woman's face pressed up against the glass on the driver's-side door and I looked right into her eyes as she slid off; they were wide and bloodshot - pleading or murderous, I couldn't tell which. And I noticed something else... Then she was gone again, replaced by another body - but I was facing front again, watching out for more craters.

None came, but I saw in my mirror that huge cracks were spreading from that hole - reminded me a little of the glass back at the facility, and I knew what came after that.

In this case, it was so much worse.

The cracks reached the buildings on either side of that street, one in particular which looked like a law court or something, then up the sides of them. Eyes flitting from the crowds in front to the rear view, I saw enormous zig-zag streaks travelling up those buildings. It sent shudders along the road, which again I felt through the tyres and the metal of the car's frame.

I stamped on the accelerator, trying not to care as I rammed into more of the affected. One barrelled over the bonnet and smacked against the windscreen, splintering it. For a few moments I was completely blind, until the shape rolled off again... and I had to swerve quickly to avoid a collision with a wall.

That was the least of my problems, though, because just behind me the buildings were starting to topple. Only one at first, but then another and another. They came crashing down as surely as if they'd been marked for demolition - falling on top of many of the affected, crushing them so completely I didn't feel guilty anymore about driving through them. The collapsed buildings were causing more cracks to appear in the road, chasing me just like the affected had done.

The bridge... I had to get to the bridge. I couldn't be that far away from it, either. I had to be nearly there, had to be...

Then I saw it, like a mirage in the desert - the way out. I coaxed more speed from the car, shrugging off any stragglers I'd picked up along the way that might be slowing me down. There was a cloud of dust and smoke hounding me now as well, from the felled buildings, threatening to overtake me and make me blind again. The ground was still shaking as I revved the engine and made it up and onto the bridge. Looking back I saw the cracks outrun the dust, starting to creep onto the bridge itself.

"Bollocks!" I hissed through my teeth.

If the bridge went at that end, I'd definitely go with it. There were no more affected attached to the car anymore, and I couldn't see any behind me for the plumes - but I could still only go so fast.

I was almost halfway across by the time the bridge started to collapse. I felt the car begin to tilt, nose upwards, but could do nothing except carry on and hope for the best. The car's engine was protesting, but I pushed it further - praying the momentum would get me across. It wasn't like the movies, where I could do some sort of stuntman leap to get me over. This was more of a leap of faith, if anything.

By the time I was almost at the other side, the car was on an incline and the bridge was rapidly disintegrating behind me. If I made it over, at least none of the affected would be chasing me - those who'd crawled out of the rubble, anyway. I admit, I closed my eyes for the final push - waiting for gravity to drag me backwards, and for the car to fall into the river below. And it was quite a fall: maybe not enough to kill me outright, but I had no idea how deep the water was, or whether I'd be able to swim out from the wreckage even if I survived the drop.

In the end, I didn't have to find out. When I opened my eyes again, I was on the other side - the collapse of the bridge having stopped just shy of my side. I was on an even keel now, heading on up the road and away from the bridge... from the town itself. The more distance I put between it and me the better - and when I looked in the mirror again, all I could see was death and destruction.

That, although I didn't really know it at the time, would be the theme for this new world. They would be my constant companions on my journey, and the predators always at my back.

Stop.

CHAPTER FIVE

Record:

Been a week or so since my last entry, and the other night I listened to the previous couple - as I tend to do, picking up the thread again. But my Lord, what state of mind must I have been in when I signed off...? All that poetic crap about death and destruction, like they were people. They're not. They're just a way of... I was going to say way of life, but there's very little about the world around me that's *living* any more. Existing, maybe; no more than that. Going backwards, definitely.

It's been a week, because not only did I want to put in a good bit of travelling in during that time, I also couldn't face telling any more of the story. Got me down to be honest... Ha - got me down... What exactly gets me *up* these days? And I mean that literally, in that I find it a real struggle to get myself moving and on the road again in the mornings.

But anyway, my problem - and I do need to carry on with this. It might even help get things straight in my head; might help me figure out the 'why' of it all. Move on, as I've said, not just physically but mentally as well. So, here we go again. I've found an isolated spot, with good visibility in every direction; it'll do until I've finished with the next leg of the journal anyway.

We'd got to the bridge, hadn't we; the escape from that town. I managed to put a fair few miles between me and that shit-hole before the car started to splutter, then eventually break down. Wasn't fuel - because again, like the chopper, according to the gauge I had almost a full tank - so it must have been wear and tear. Couldn't really blame it, I suppose - I'd put it through its paces back there. Still, it would leave me stranded out in the middle of nowhere once more. Not a bad situation given the alternative, of being back in an urban environment with potential killers around every turn, but I wondered if I could get *that* moving and on the road again. My little joke...

Now, I don't know much beyond the basics of engines. I can drive, I can fly, but what keeps those machines ticking is very much beyond me. Used to watch the engineers back in my Air Force days, flitting about, seeing to the maintenance of those planes and helicopters. They were like magicians, some of them, could make each part do wonders... Or like conductors in an orchestra, encouraging each section to work and make the whole thing produce the sweetest of music. And there we were, abusing their darlings - treating them so badly. Bit like in real life, I suppose; the aircraft even had female names.

Point is, I would have given anything for someone on that deserted road who knew one end of a carburettor from the other. Wasn't as if I could just get the AA on the phone to come out and give me a tow - more's the pity. The AA had probably by now killed one other or screwed themselves senseless. I had to face the fact that I was on my own, and if I was to fix the Ford I was going to have to learn on the job. Might just be something as simple as a fan belt, in which case I could probably find something to replace it with... but where was a good old-fashioned stocking when you needed one?

I popped the bonnet and climbed out to take a look. Lifting it and securing it, I took a gander at the engine itself - and immediately saw what the problem was. In spite of how new the paintwork on the car appeared, what was keeping it running - or not, as the case turned out to be - was dotted with rust. A *kind* of rust, at any rate - coppery in colour, flaky and patchy, it reminded me a little of the mould at some of the hostels I'd stayed in during my adventures abroad. I reached out and prodded a piece that was coating the motor. My fingers brushed it and I watched as it crumbled under my touch - leaving a small hole in the casing. I might not have known that much about engines, but I knew I wasn't going to be fixing this one in a hurry; I was lucky it had got me off that bridge, let alone this far.

Except now that I stepped away from under the bonnet, I saw patches on the car's side of that same stuff - originating from the tyre well. There were a few more spots towards the back on the flank as well. I stood there and frowned. Everything had happened in a bit of a rush, especially after the affected began congregating to chase after me - that kind of mass panic mode Carrie had talked about in the cellar - but I could have sworn the rust hadn't been there when we set off. I'd chosen the car specifically because it looked like it would get me away from town; as fast as possible, in fact - that and it happened to start, of course. So what...?

Something began to spark in my mind: a recollection. But I didn't have time to think about it, to piece things together - not at that time.

Largely because of the birds...

I heard the things before I even saw them, though Christ knows how; there were so many. You just get used to birdsong, tune it out, but the racket they were making was something else. All weirdly out of tune; squawking more than singing. Some sounded as if they were in pain, others like they were laughing - and there were so many of the buggers when I looked up. They were like a big black cloud in the sky, but moving too quickly; not taking their time like clouds drifting across the horizon. The closer they came, the more I could see that they were made up of different types and sizes - birds who would never normally flock together at all: blackbirds with sparrows; pigeons and starlings... The way they were flying was erratic, too. Some were striking each other in mid-air, knocking their neighbours out of the way, or pecking at them.

Then they banked. It wasn't fluid, wasn't like those displays the Red Arrows used to put on that Dad would take me to see - fuelling my interest in all things aircraft-related - but clumsy and haphazard, like trying to turn a horse-drawn cart too quickly. I watched all this, puzzled, then realised the banking was growing steeper - that the flock was heading in my direction. It still took me a few moments to shake myself out of my stupor - part of me wanting to carry on observing, another part screaming that I needed to get the hell out of there right now!

By the time I'd started moving, the birds were already dive-bombing. Some crashed into the ground not far from me, some struck the car - just as I was ducking down to use it as a shield. They hit the vehicle with such force it was like shells punching into it, smashing glass and metal alike. Several flew straight down into the roof, then through it on impact. Down they plummeted, but they also began to fly around me, circling the car to peck, to stab at me. The combination of my clothes and the SKIN protected me from the worst of it, but there were just so many to fight off. I managed to get the car door open, slide across and grab the rifle and my bag. I laid down a spray of bullets - but when I got out of the car and stood upright, I just waved the weapon back and forth like a mad woman with a broom, batting at cobwebs.

Hitchcock had nothing on these bastards, I tell you. They didn't care whether they lived or died - as the Kamikaze ones still raining down proved. All they wanted was to attack me, to cause as much havoc as they possibly could. Through the flurry of wings and beaks, I spotted a wood in the distance. They'd follow me, no doubt, but if I made it to the trees I'd at least have more cover than I had standing there.

So, shouldering the backpack and gun, I put up my arms as a barrier and ran. I ploughed through them, just as I had with the affected and the car in town. But I soon realised that these poor creatures were just as messed up as the humans back where I'd come from, just as corrupted by whatever it was that had done this.

Visibility was worse than it had been when that guy had landed on my windscreen, or when the dust cloud was chasing me to the bridge. Only this time I felt more exposed, if that makes sense, regardless of the fact I still had some protection – I was enclosed inside a different kind of bubble, not of metal but of the SKIN's making. That run seemed to take forever, with birds crashing into me from behind, from in front and above. It would only have taken one to drop dead centre on me, and I'd have been done – but I kept on moving, heading forwards, heading onwards. Until I finally reached the treeline.

I almost ran slap-bang into the trunk of one tree, in fact – only at the last moment diving sideways and letting my feathered 'friends' have that privilege. The further into the wood I went, the less the birds followed me. Then, at last, when it felt like I was never going to be rid of them, or would run out of trees in the process, they were gone – almost as suddenly as they'd appeared in the first place.

Leaning back against a trunk, I slumped down and got my breath back. I couldn't even assume I was safe out here in the countryside now; absolutely anything could turn against me. And I saw that again when I came out of the woods, spotting a couple of cows in a nearby field that were butting heads in a fight to the death. I couldn't help thinking of that disease in the late twentieth century, how people had been so scared of meat from 'mad' cows in case it infected them. These were the real deal, and it made me wonder if perhaps all this had happened because of contaminated food or drink instead of being carried in the air? Or maybe it had mutated from that? It was pointless to speculate, but I wanted – *needed* – answers, and I wasn't about to get them out there.

As I trudged away from the trees, avoiding insane livestock, I kept turning to look up at the sky in case those birds found me again and I needed to break for more cover. Didn't happen, though, and it wasn't long before I saw a farm in the distance – probably the one that the cows belonged to. I headed off that way, figuring it was worth checking out. Maybe I'd find more people who hadn't been plagued by the psychosis, but mostly it was because the sky was darkening, about to rain, and I wanted somewhere to shelter - silly really, because I couldn't even get wet; but then a lot of mental hang-ups were still left from before the time I put on the SKIN. Still are.

The property looked deserted - perhaps it had been before all this, because I saw it was quite run down the nearer I got. *Falling down* might have been a more accurate description, especially for the outhouses and barns, and I had a flashback to those buildings in town that had toppled because of the craters, because of the cracks in the road. We don't get earthquakes much in this country; extremely rare. And never ones which do that kind of damage. Was it just a coincidence it had happened around the same time as the madness, or something more? My mind was still racing; I needed to rest.

The farmhouse itself looked like the best bet out of the lot; built from stone, it appeared stable enough. The door was open, so I went inside - gun raised in case of trouble. I moved through the kitchen, through the hall, then into the living room - where I found an old man sitting in a chair. Damn, he looked so much like Dad, that guy. Even more so because he'd clearly died there and no-one had come looking. No bottles of milk for the neighbours to see; no neighbours for miles, come to that. He'd just passed away and was rotting, skin grey and mottled, head back and his mouth wide.

In his lap, open at the page he'd been reading, was a Bible - and as I looked around the room, wrenching my eyes away from him, I saw there were various crosses and framed religious passages. I returned my gaze to the corpse, taking a step or two. But I didn't want to see the sections he'd been reading in that book, because of what I feared they might be; didn't want to look upstairs - not just because the steps seemed as rickety as all hell, but because I was frightened of seeing something... *someone* in the bed. Maybe a wizened old woman, his wife. Not saying that makes any sense - and I probably should have made sure there were no nasty surprises - but it did to me at the time.

So I simply sat down opposite the man and continued to stare at him.

As I did that, suddenly things started to take shape. I remembered what I'd seen when that woman had pressed her face up against the driver's side window. Something spreading up her neck, across her face - like the rust on the car, but slightly different: dead skin, like that of the man's in front of me. No, not just dead... decaying. The same was true of those birds on the ground, I now recalled. Some of them bald in places - which could have been due to the hard landing, yet something told me it wasn't. Flashes of things in my head, connections being made. This man, my father, the woman's face... The birds, the crazy people, Mum... The buildings outside that were in such a state of disrepair, and those falling buildings again... The hole in the motor, the holes in the road... flaking, cracking.

And then, I guess you could say I had a revelation. I knew what was happening, even if I didn't know the reason for it. Everything - like this man, whether he'd died of natural causes or not; like my Dad had been after he'd taken his own life - was rotting away. The craziness that had been caused back in the facility, back in that town, had happened because the rot had somehow wormed its way into people's brains - affecting them in the same way that terrible disease had affected my mother and so many others I'd witnessed when she'd been taken in. Maybe it had crept up the back, into the brain-stem - something that wasn't visible straight away, something you had to *look for* specifically. It would explain the different kinds of behaviour anyway... and did you know - I certainly didn't until I found out later on - that a bird's brain and a human brain have similar wiring?

And brains, like machines - like a car or helicopter engine, or even a gun - only have to have one faulty, one malfunctioning part for the whole thing to go to pot. But it hadn't just got into people, into machinery this... this *Rot*. It had got into the roads, buildings. Organic, non-organic. As incredible as it sounded, it was fucking up everything around us. I couldn't prove any of this at that time, of course – for that I would need to do some research, maybe find books that could help, do some tests, but it all made sense to me. For the first time since I'd heard the alarms, that gunfire back at the facility, it all made perfect sense!

I don't know at what point after I'd been thinking all this I dropped to sleep, but it was like my body needed to recharge, and now I'd reached this conclusion it could power down for a while. I remember dreaming about clouds again, about flying. No cats woke me up this time, however, I just opened my eyes when the sun came flooding in through the window, finding us in that living room. It had the capacity to make anything look beautiful, that light – another thing we all took for granted, every day – even that dead farmer, who looked so peaceful in his chair. I hoped then he'd gone before all this took hold, before the Rot did something to his brain; to his land. Probably hadn't... but it did tell me one thing: that this fucking disease didn't re-animate the dead. No people rising out of their graves to eat you in this apocalypse, thank fuck. So, you will never hear me say the 'Z-word', no matter what state these people find themselves in. Just doesn't describe them. Dying, putrefying, but not dead.

I thought about burying him, saying a few words, but it seemed cruel to move him. This was his home, probably had been forever, and it felt right to cremate him inside it. Felt also like the fire would be doing something good this time, something cleansing instead of killing people as it had done at the facility; in the cellar. Out the back, I found a couple of tractors that didn't look like they'd been used in an age – although in this new climate, how could you tell? – but I also found cans, some of which still had diesel inside. I spent the next twenty minutes or so pouring it onto stuff inside, starting with the old man, and then I dug out some matches from the kitchen.

As I walked away from that farm, leaving it burning up, I said a quick prayer for the man who had looked so much like my father – or like he would have looked before the undertakers cleaned him up. Wondered if there really had been a wife upstairs in the bedroom.

Wondered what I would find when I reached the next town or city.

Stop.

CHAPTER SIX

Record:

Once I knew about it, once I knew what to look for – instead of my eyes sliding off it; my mind filtering it out – I saw it everywhere on my journey. For example, I came across a lake covered in patches of what I thought was algae. Not all that unusual, you might think, but there was just something about this particular stuff. Wasn't green for a start, it was a kind of purple-grey colour. I found a stick and poked at one of the denser bits, which wrapped itself around the wood. Sure enough, when I brought it out again, it was already starting to be eaten away, like I'd just dipped it in acid. I knew the SKIN would probably protect me even from this, but I wasn't willing to put it to the test until I had no choice. Instead, I threw a stone into the centre of the lake, urging the water, the ripples, to tear into that Rot – to break it up. Did very little good; the infection was too strong and spreading all the time. But I had to believe there was a way to fix this, to fight it, to reverse it. That there was still hope.

I headed south, following my compass until I hit a main road and then a motorway. Sticking to hills which ran parallel to the long road, some of which were covered with grass that was turning brown – dying or already dead – I saw cars that had been either abandoned or their drivers had crashed them. Thought about going down and seeing if any would start, but it was too much hassle. The affected were flitting between them; some even crawling over lorries or coaches, as I hunkered down on the hillside and watched them through my binoculars. Each person, and every vehicle down there, was in a different stage of the Rot. With some figures it had accelerated, now covering half their faces, eating away the flesh in parts – so that I could see teeth and tongues through their cheeks. With others it was only noticeable if you looked really hard; tiny islands of Rot at the hairline – which wasn't to say it hadn't covered other parts of their bodies, beneath whatever clothing they had on. It at least backed up the idea that the virus spread at different speeds in different cases.

I saw more cracks in the roads as well, holes ranging in size from the crater-like one I'd seen before to some as small as hubcaps. The closer I came to the city this road was guiding me to, the more I could see how the virus had devastated the buildings. There was an office block, for instance, which had Rot climbing up the side like ivy up a cottage; here and there its insides had been exposed, displaying rooms with desks and chairs rather than organs and muscles – but the effect was the same.

I made a conscious decision there and then never to go up higher than the first floor of a building, and even then to be ready to make my exit quickly in case of tremors. Nothing that we had trusted before could be relied on now, and I thought to myself, *does that include reality?* This was all so alien to me, like the Rot was transforming our landscape into one of those distant planets the SKIN was designed for… and that made me wonder whether the cause had really been man-made at all? Chemical weapons we concocted ourselves, or some race out there in the heavens trying to destroy us for whatever purposes. Science fiction or cold, hard facts? After all, nothing *should* be able to affect organic and non-organic material in the same way.

As I crested one of the last hills before I hit that sprawling metropolis, I caught sight of a stadium. Obviously used for sporting events at one time, football matches and athletics, it had probably also hosted its fair share of concerts. That was something I hadn't even thought about while I'd been on this trek: how much I missed music. Still do, though I've managed to find a working iPod here and there since then – working for a little while, at any rate, so I can listen to songs through the speakers. Anyway, that place was full of the affected – the

Rotten, as I've since come to call them. Filling the stands, covering the grounds; it was clearly where they had chosen to gather - maybe following the call of some kind of trace memory from their previous lives? Somewhere they went to have a good time? Would explain why we kept hearing them above us in the pub, why they kept coming back time and again - I'm still surprised they weren't there when I went upstairs.

Mum was always trying to get out of the house when the dementia really started to kick in. Trying to get somewhere, though she could never explain exactly where. Then, inside the specialist ward they'd taken her to - I'm loath to call it a home, because the place was like Fort Knox - while she was still in better shape than she had been in that hospital bed, she'd wandered the corridors convinced she was walking the streets of her old village where she grew up. Perhaps that was it, going to somewhere comforting; that made you feel better? Often she'd gather other patients as she went, like the Pied Piper. All of them seeking something together - though at times it would also lead to fighting amongst themselves.

I was witnessing a similar kind of behaviour now, droves of the Rotten flocking together like those birds, to go somewhere - to do something they couldn't explain even to themselves. Congregating to listen to some sort of unspoken sermon. Was that where they'd been in the last town, while I wandered through deserted streets? After an initial spurt of energy, had they calmed down and followed some kind of call - only to realise at the last minute I was trying to get away? Pretty egotistical of me! Did it really make any difference now? Did their behaviour since it all happened matter? Surely the only thing that did was getting to the bottom of 'how', and putting a stop to it. Returning things to the way they had been before... Even more arrogant, you might say, but I still had to try; for all I knew there *was* only me.

Waiting for cover of darkness this time, and using the night-vision scope to see, I slipped into the city as stealthily as I could. My gun was primed, and - so far - not suffering from any effects of the Rot. But I wasn't relying solely on that anyway, as I had the hammer and hatchet tucked into my belt, just in case. My first port of call would be a Tourist Information Centre, something with detailed maps of the city.... Of course, they don't make maps to help you find *those* places, but eventually I came across a signpost pointing to one - Rot only partially obscuring the letters. It was deserted inside, as far as I could tell, and I found what I was looking for quickly, tucking a dozen or so into my backpack - I figured it wouldn't hurt to have spares in case any of them should fall to pieces.

The map told me my next port of call was on the east side of town, a straight line from the Tourist Information - so I just had to keep heading in that direction to hit it. I was about halfway there when I felt the now familiar rumblings of the earth - followed by a building collapse maybe a few streets away. It urged me on to my destination - to get what I needed as quickly as possible - assuming that was still standing, of course.

It was. The library, being an old building that had already stood the test of time, would probably still be standing when everything else had crumbled around it... I hoped. There were none of the Rotten inside here, either, which was a sad testament to how things were before; the fact fewer and fewer people were going to them, how many were shutting down. But I still didn't want to hang around, so I set to work looking for the section I needed: the sciences. Now, I've never been one for studying - not really. A lot of what I learned to be a pilot was a necessity, but the skills were already there. Didn't mean I *couldn't* learn, though - I'm not stupid by any stretch of the imagination. Nevertheless, some of that stuff made my head hurt, seriously.

I grabbed what I considered essential and got out of there as fast as possible - heading back to the outskirts of the city, up onto those hills where I knew I'd be relatively safe. That was where I flipped through those books, studying information about how things are made up, about genetics and cell structure and diseases – lots of things I've already forgotten about. Was no mystery what put me to sleep the following night, that's all I'm saying.

What the books seemed to be telling me about establishing the nature of viruses, was that I had to study a range of samples from different sources under a microscope. Any school worth their salt would have dozens of those – but to examine anything at the magnification I needed, I'd have to visit a hospital or university. I'd have to take that risk.

St August's was on the far side of town, apparently, so I skirted round and came at it from the back. Had to be in the day this time, because I couldn't rely on finding a working electron microscope or the power being on – and an optical one would require light. As luck would have it I was wrong on both counts about the electron. Trust me, I wasn't complaining. Like the library, St August's was pretty much empty; I guess nobody was in a rush to head to a hospital, either voluntarily or in great numbers. I did spot a few of the Rotten outside, hanging around as if they didn't really know what to do with themselves, but they didn't stay long before wandering off again.

Under the microscope, I scrutinised my samples: the first, metal from an abandoned scooter; the second, a scraping from the side of a building; and the third, part of a weed growing by the side of the road. All proved without a shadow of a doubt what I'd been thinking: that the material – organic or inorganic – was breaking down, and at different rates. The same thing was attacking what was holding each of them together, causing them to lose their coherence. In the case of the weed's cells, the structure was shifting even as I watched, some sort of bacteria breaking through the protective membrane. By the time I came to take it out again, it had already pretty much rotted away.

Time to look at a human sample... from one of the

Rotten. It was the only way to know exactly what we were dealing with, to either prevent or cure those suffering from it. And by Christ, were they suffering, whether they realised it or not. Their own bodies turning against them, forcing them to turn on each other. In order to take a look at skin and blood samples from a living host, though, I would have to catch one...

To get my sample would mean going where I knew they would be. Probably not the stadium - I didn't fancy taking on so many, just to capture one. Places like the library and St August's were not good hunting grounds, as I'd discovered; not areas the vast majority of the population wanted to be, even unconsciously. There was a shopping centre not too far away, though - somewhere these dispossessed people might gravitate towards, I reasoned, but spread out. A place where I might be able to grab one of the Rotten and subdue them before the rest even realised what was happening. Worth scoping out at any rate, which is what I did next.

I found a vantage point where I could spy on the shops, see just how many of the Rotten might be coming or going. At first I couldn't see any at all, just the after-effects of the incident; of the Rot itself. There was a chemist's, which had a huge picture of a woman's face in the window, selling some sort of beauty product or other. The chemicals we used to put on our skin, just to stop the signs of ageing, or make-up to look better... But that was nothing compared to the chemicals we put *inside* ourselves; pills for this, pills for that - even if you didn't need to take them. Had all of that shit contributed towards what had happened? I wondered. It seemed apt, therefore, that half the woman's face in the display was now covered with the Rot, mirroring what was happening to the populace in general.

But still no sign of any...

Then I saw him, a lone Rotten - rake thin and dressed in black clothing, shuffling through the square between shops. The man had his back to me, moving very slowly, raising his hands in the air every now and again as if he'd just had some kind of Eureka moment, shouting something I couldn't hear from this distance. I did a quick check around, and the coast was still clear apart from him. I probably thought I was being given a gift here, a Godsend – someone I could just go down there and whack on the head; carry off to the hospital over my shoulder while it was all quiet on the Western front. Looked positively laid back compared to some I'd seen and encountered; if I played this just right then no mess, no fuss.

Didn't quite pan out that way. I crept down, hoping the man hadn't vanished by the time I reached the square. No, there he was, just standing around – raising his hands every now and again, muttering under his breath now, the odd word raised. I had a moment where I thought maybe he was one of those who hadn't come down with this, like Carrie, Rakesh or Dennis, but then I saw the back of his neck, saw the telltale spread of the disease that had infected his mind as well as his body. Nodding to myself, and looking left and right – one final check that there were no more of his brethren around – I ran out into the square.

The nearer I got to him, the more I could make out what he was saying. The mutterings were random, but I could hear words every now and again:

"Shameful deed... mercy... cleanse... joy..." Then the big one: "Lord our Father!" That was shouted at the top of his lungs. I paused; the rifle butt raised and ready to bop him in the head. Couldn't do it, though; just couldn't.

It was at that moment he turned, and I saw why he was dressed in black: the dog collar, hanging from the top his shirt, no longer fixed in place, but still giving away what this man had been before the Rot set in. Quite literally a Godsend.

His eyes were darting around all over the place, but they kept rolling up to the sky as if imploring his Saviour to do something about his condition.

"Sinner!" he shouted, pointing. Then louder. "*Sinner!*"

I was frozen, could do nothing. When he started screaming the word, I actually tried to shush him - but it was already too late. His Lord might not have answered his call, but the other Rotten had, and suddenly I was aware of figures all around, emerging from the shops that had looked so vacant from my place of safety. Just who was the hunter now? Whether intentionally or not, a trap had been set for me - this man of the cloth the bait. And suddenly I was surrounded by Rotten of every shape and size, all coming towards me.

I turned my gun on the nearest to my left, a man who was wearing what looked like underpants on his head - probably from the clothing shop he'd ventured out of. But as ridiculous as his appearance might be, his mannerisms were completely the opposite: fists raised and ready to pummel me into next week.

"Get back!" I warned, not really knowing why I was bothering. They didn't - couldn't - understand me anymore. Didn't even care half the time if you hurt them, shot them. Not that it made it any easier for me to do.

I aimed downwards, shooting a kneecap out and watching him fall to the ground. Didn't stop him, though, and he continued to crawl towards me, leaving a trail of blood behind him like the slime of a snail. Someone to my right now, hands grabbing my backpack; I whirled and fired again... A woman this time, maybe in her '30s, the top half of her dress torn away, flabby breasts exposed and covered in Rot. The bullet at that close range sent her reeling backwards and into two more of her kind.

As affected as he was, the priest had been right - I was a sinner. I was a murderer. But I'd been left very little choice. I fired a spray into the crowd that was massing, no time to aim now - no time to take the softly, softly approach.

One of the Rotten was charging towards me with his

head down, like a human battering ram. I aimed the gun and pulled back on the trigger.

Nothing happened.

Whether I'd finally run out of bullets or the weapon had succumbed to the Rot, I had no way of knowing, but it left me defenceless in the moment. That guy's head slammed into me, and the effect was like a bull charging, tossing its victims on its horns. My rifle went clattering off who knows where. When I landed, I saw stars - then immediately felt feet kicking me, as several of the Rotten crowded in. Shaking my head, I got up onto one elbow and managed to reach round to my belt for the hammer. Someone's face loomed in, man or woman I couldn't tell which, a cascade of saliva drooling down their chin, and I whacked them with my new weapon - not hard, certainly not hard enough to warrant what happened. The whole of their chin came away with the head of the hammer, leaving just a tongue to dart in and out. In their case, the Rot must have weakened the flesh and bone there to such an extent it was like the road, the buildings; the slightest knock and it turned to mulch.

Wasn't so for the elbow which caught me a glancing blow to the temple - that was solid enough. I had to get out of there, before they started to pile in on top and crush me, but the Rotten weren't allowing me enough room to move, let alone get up. I had to think, and think fast.

When you can't go forward or back, then I guess the only thing to do is go sideways. So I began rolling; not easy when you have a backpack on, but actually that only helped to knock the feet out from under the Rotten. They started to go down like pins in a bowling alley, and by the time I came to a stop I'd made a channel in the crowd. Enough to scramble to my feet at least, drawing the small hatchet at the same time and planting that in the shoulder of the nearest Rotten figure. That guy tugged it away and out of my hands, so I lashed out at two more with the hammer.

Then I ran.

My dad taught me when I was little not to be afraid of bullies, that even if people were bigger and stronger than you when you fought back they would inevitably crumble - *actually* crumble in the case of some of the Rotten. But he also taught me the value of beating a hasty retreat in the face of superior numbers. I could stand up to Colin Drakes when he was trying to take my pocket money if he was on his own, but if he had his mates with him - Kenny Thompson and Mark Platts - if the Three Stooges were all together, then it was time to get the fuck out of the back alley.

In this instance, the alleys were the first places I headed for. I could thin out the Rottens' numbers in those, lose them in the warrens of the city's back streets which I'd studied on those maps. It was like the birds and the woods; eventually they stopped chasing me. But I'd failed, and failed miserably to get a live test subject.

Then I looked down at the hammer, at the gore that was still dripping from it. I had all the samples I needed on that thing. I'd just scrape some off and stick them under the 'scope, then I'd see who the real enemy was. The biggest and strongest bully I needed to tackle.

So I made my way back out to the hospital - taking care to keep the hammer away from anything that might contaminate it. Or contaminate it more than it already had been. I was almost at St August's when there was another rumble, another 'quake. I could do nothing but watch as cracks appeared in the road ahead of me, and a much larger one reached the hospital building itself - raced up the side of it. Cracking like an egg, the structure began to destabilise. Then the building collapsed in on itself, was sucked into the ground, taking the microscope and any hopes of studying the new samples with it.

I should have been grateful that I wasn't inside at the time the whole thing went, but I just swore at the sky - swearing at the very deity the holy man had been imploring. Yes, I could start again I supposed. Try and find another microscope somewhere here, or even move on to another place, another hospital. But what was the point? What was the point in any of it...? I was no doctor, no scientist. I had a rough idea what I was doing, but who was I kidding? I couldn't fix this.

Dropping to my knees not far away from all the rubble, I just stared at what had once been St August's, hanging my head in disbelief.

I stayed there until it grew dark again, then I just sat and waited for the dawn.

Stop.

CHAPTER SEVEN

Record:

Seemed like a good place to leave it for a little while, that, me sitting and gazing out at a heap of rubble. Almost poetic, isn't it? Romantic – the sun coming up again and bathing everything in its light.

Wasn't like that, believe me. You had to be there, you had to have felt the bitterness, the despondency and self-pity – worse than ever before. Wasn't just the dawn, it was the dawning realisation that I was powerless in the face of this thing. That if I hadn't been wearing the SKIN I'd probably be like the rest of those sad fuckers, wearing my shorts on my head and pissing myself... oh, wait, I do that anyway on a regular basis.

God, I miss having a drink. Having something to eat. Sometimes I hallucinate about a nice juicy burger, fries, and a coke. Drive-throughs were a thing of beauty and don't let anyone ever tell you otherwise... Oh, and pizza delivery.

No, I'm just driving myself crazy with all this shit. Not going to happen. I need to get on with the story, because we've almost caught up to the present. Not much more to go with it, then I'll decide whether or not to carry on after that. I haven't really made my mind up about what to do... not about carrying on the record, but about where to go from here. There...

Look, I'll start this again some other time.

I'm tired.

Pause.

Resume recording:

You know me too well; I couldn't just leave it there once I'd started.

Moving on again, just like I did after the collapse of the hospital. If it hadn't been for another thought, okay another *revelation* if you like, I'd probably have stalled for good there and then. But something I'd read in those books kept coming back to me, time and time again, about how outbreaks were dealt with in the past. About getting the most information from 'Ground Zero,' where the virus first occurred. That could tell you much more than any of this dicking around I was doing.

Right, it's like the ripples on the lake again, or the glass splintering on the car windscreen, the glass back at the facility. Once I'd made that connection, once I'd thought about it... Dennis, you see; he was the one who threw me off track, had me covering up and pretending I'd come from a hospital, when in fact I'd come from a place where they were experimenting with all kinds of crap. Denied it so often that I think I'd started believing it myself, and I suppose I was in no real hurry to go back there - too many bad memories. Like going back to the scene of a crime.

But that's where the crack first appeared for me. Not just in the glass window of my room, but when I first heard the alarms, first saw that guard shooting up the place. I had no proof, of course, that anything had originated there - if it had, then the bloody thing spread quickly, and spread everywhere. You know how it is, though, once you get an idea in your head - and it was something to motivate me.

I needed that.

I'd get moving, but not forward this time, I'd retrace my steps. Go back along the motorway I'd followed here, back to Miccleston, and from there the facility - which in its own way might take me forwards, I told myself. Whatever - it was better than just mooching around and waiting for the end to come. Something positive I *could* do, and in time that would become my sole focus.

Picking myself up, I started the next leg. I thought about trying to preserve the hammer, but by the time I got back 'home' it wouldn't be a fresh sample anyway - plus I figured I might need it. That and the fold-up saw were the only weapons I had left on me... when I set off, that was. Gathered a few more as I went. For instance, it took me off the track a little, but I came across this old castle while I was walking - one of those places that would have been a tourist attraction at one time, but had probably closed its doors long before the Rot. It was another risk getting so close, but I could see through the windows that there were displays of old medieval weaponry behind glass cases. Hard to tell whether the castle had been affected yet, because it was so old and in such a state - but I broke in anyway and quickly grabbed what I could, bundling up armfuls of the things and running off over the hill with them like a kid stealing sweets.

When I was far enough away to be sure that the castle wasn't going to fall down on top of me, I sat and went through my spoils. They included a rather lethal-looking mace, which had a ball covered in spikes on one end, a sword, and an axe that put its little brother I'd lost in the city brawl to shame. Not that I didn't come across guns on my travels, it was just that I tended to see those old kinds of weapons as more reliable. Less parts that needed to work than a gun, y'know? - although even these could let you down at the last moment. I remember one time when I came up against a Rotten and I had this—

Oh, right, back on point. More reliable anyway, especially back then. I didn't encounter too much trouble from the Rotten, anyway - tried to avoid them as much as possible, staying out of the population centres and sticking to the countryside, which itself was changing all around me from day to day. Less and less green and more brown and grey, as everything turned - some stuff slowly, some more quickly. I saw some weird shit on that journey, I can tell you. An entire wood like the one I'd taken cover from the birds in... might have been the same one, even, I'd just come at it from a different angle. But anyway, I saw that entire wood just start to sink gradually into the ground, one tree after the next. Some stopped when they got to the branches, some were just dragged right under, as their roots and the soil around the trunks failed them.

Another time, I saw a row of pylons - and one of them must have rusted away at the leg, causing it to topple over. But because they were all attached, it took the others with it. Metal giants, all tumbling one after the other like dominoes. Nobody had seen anything like it before and I guess nobody ever will again. Only me. I didn't know whether to feel honoured or cursed. Probably a bit of both.

I also managed to narrowly avoid a stampede of horses, which came trampling over a hill. Again, typical of the behaviour of those *actually* cursed by the Rot, they were travelling together but not really, if you see what I mean. Their condition varied, as with everything else; some looked like they had only just started to show symptoms of the disease, while others were positively ravaged by it - I saw exposed ribs on the sides of some, bones at the legs, and skulls shining through thinning flesh. None would have looked out of place carrying the Four Horsemen and in fact I had to quickly check that the lead ones weren't. I wouldn't have been at all surprised, and it just made me think again about that old farmer who looked like Dad... who'd had his Bible open at a certain page.

I didn't walk all the way, though. More than once, when I had been really exhausted, I set out to look for a car or something that might carry me a little further; most packed up after only a mile or so, if they even started in the first place, but it was better than nothing. Found a really nice black Lexmoto bike outside one tiny village - it had probably belonged to someone who had been trying to compensate for something, but I wasn't complaining, especially as it still fired up. Reminded me a bit of the one I used to own when I was rocking up to test those planes.

Should have left the bike where it was, mind. When that packed up, it sent me skidding into a ditch - head over heels. Adrenalin junkie that I am, I couldn't keep the speed down on that thing, and it cost me. I thought for a minute it had cost me my protection, the SKIN - that maybe the tumble had perforated the suit. Stupid, stupid... I was lucky, however. Got away with just a few bruises, but it could have been so much worse. What if I'd broken a leg or an arm? There were no doctors around to set it, and even if there were, they would have had to take off the SKIN to do it properly. Making my way through this environment was dangerous enough without putting myself in such situations. Took me a few days to recover from that, and I walked pretty much all the way afterwards. Limped to start with.

I admit, I got lost a few times, in spite of the fact I was just heading in a straight line after I passed Miccleston. At one point I realised I'd got turned around, when I came across the same set of drystone walls I'd passed a few days previously - only they were in a much worse state when I found them again, collapsing in any number of spots. My compass was all but useless by now, just kept spinning round and round, so I had to just follow my nose.

Took what felt like weeks to get back there, but when I saw that fencing - which was actually still in quite good shape - it was honestly like the most beautiful thing I'd ever clapped eyes on; even better than the sun. If only the rest of that place had been in such good nick.

The grounds were deserted, and the bodies that had fallen there had been rotting away all this time, becoming a part of the concrete or what was left of the grass. What the fire hadn't consumed, the Rot had taken. The structure of the building itself was still there, which amazed me, but it bore only a passing resemblance to the place I'd been taken to in the middle of the night; more like some sort of monument to the events that had happened there. Wasn't somewhere I wanted to go inside, but I was still thinking then that maybe there'd be something in there which could help with my quest. My fight. So I ventured in, the glass at the doors having either smashed or melted away a long time ago, allowing me easy access.

I trod carefully through a blackened foyer, the building as forsaken as the grounds outside. Hardly surprising, though – if anyone had survived this, then they wouldn't have remained here all this time. Still, I kept my guard up and my mace and sword in my hands. The lifts had been one of the first things to go, so there was no use trying those, but the stairs were intact, just covered in ash. It was almost as if a battle had gone on here, Rot against the flames, each cancelling the other out – or fusing together – and I made a mental note to test that if I ever got out of there alive. Could fire actually beat back the Rot, or even absorb it? I knew it could damage those who'd been affected, but could it drive out the infection, or at the very least put a halt to it?

That wasn't why I was there. Ground zero... I needed to search each and every level to see if the Rot had actually originated in these labs, get some samples if so – though Christ knows how I thought I was going to look at them; certainly not using any of the equipment in the facility.

But on floor after floor, I found nothing but Rot and charcoal. There were holes in the walls, in the ground – and though it was anything but safe, I ignored what I'd sworn to myself and climbed higher and higher until I was at that rooftop again, the one I'd used to make my escape.

Nothing happened, there was no collapse as I made my way despondently back down again; I wouldn't have cared if it had buried me right then. There was only sadness and a sense of failure. That and a clarification. You're probably wondering how I knew exactly how long I'd been out on the road when I started these recordings. Hadn't been marking the days off or anything – what on? As I once said, couldn't trust pen or paper... or anything else, come to that. How did I know exactly *how* long?

I'll tell you fucking how. One of the only things that survived both the fire and the Rot in that whole place was the clock and calendar in my room. It was supposed to count down that week I was going to be in there, actually counted down the three days before everything went sideways.

And now, fuck me if it wasn't saying that I'd spent almost three months out there and achieved absolutely nothing. Less than nothing.

So that's where you caught me at the start, beginning the journal - as I made my way from the facility again. Living whatever existence you could call this. No idea what to do or where to go. Knowing there would be no going back, that you never could.

Just knowing this was the end of everything.

Stop.

CHAPTER EIGHT

Record:

Damn, I left that on a bit of a downer, didn't I?

Been a while, and I was at a loose end, so I played back my journal – skipped some bits, because well, they were too depressing even for me to listen to again. Even *with* this newfound hope.

I left off at the facility, going back there and discovering that – whether it was Ground Zero or not, and I still had no way of knowing it for a fact – I would get nothing from the place now. Its secrets had died with it, would *rot* with it. Oh yeah, that's right! I did test out that fire thing. Doesn't have any effect on the disease in the long run – just holds it off a little. Like the other elements, though, eventually it succumbs. Bet you've never seen fire rot, have you? I have – it's bloody terrifying and fascinating at the same time. The laws of nature get bent out of shape with this one.

Speaking of which, remember when I told you about that river and the algae? Well, not long after the facility, and in the spirit of picking myself up, dusting myself off and figuring out what to do next, I thought maybe there might be some mileage in getting off this island and making it to other shores. With that in mind, my first thought was obviously flying again – it always is. Wait, this is relevant, I'll get back to the water in a moment… Just bear with me, okay?

I'll start with the airfields. Once I'd got a bee in my bonnet about checking out the world beyond our small neck of the woods – figuring that somewhere there might just be a country that the Rot didn't reach – the best way seemed to be by air. I managed to find a few airfields and even one RAF base, which I also raided for weaponry – testing it first before taking it. Actually, testing it on some of the Rotten who were still at the base and attacked me en masse. Still up to their old tricks. On this occasion it was actually the sword which let me down. Snapping in two as I brought it round to stave off a lunge from a man whose uniform was still intact; well, enough for me to tell he'd been an officer cadet – only a young man, but his features had been raddled by the disease.

I only hesitated briefly before opening fire with the L85-A2 rifle I had slung over my shoulder, hitting him and the slew of others coming at me – grateful to have the weapon and that it was working at that particular moment. Another narrow escape, but I was getting used to them.

None of the planes I tried, either at the base or elsewhere, would start, though. Probably just as well, as the crashes in the chopper and on the motorbike might only have been a taster of things to come. I was wondering again what I had to lose really, and a short hop like that… might have been able to keep a bird in the air long enough to reach France or, going the other way, Ireland. Might also have ended up being worse than the accident that saw the end of my test-piloting career, as well. That should have put me off going up there altogether, but it never did. I was back on the horse as soon as I was able, even if it was only for pleasure.

Next on my list was by sea – which is where the river comes back into it – get to a port and maybe take a boat out. Full disclosure: I'm not much of a sailor. When I was a kid I'd get seasick going on the pedal boats at the beach, although I'd gotten over that particular weakness as I'd grown into adulthood. Again, I reckoned I'd be able to get a small boat across the ocean to one of those countries – although what I hadn't reckoned on was the state of the ocean itself, nor the effect it might have on a boat's hull. Stupid really, having seen what it did to that stick I poked into the 'algae'.

At one dock I visited, the boats tied up to the dock were

in the process of being devoured by patches of Rot - the fronts tipped up into the air, as the backs were decimated. Never could get the hang of which was bow and which stern... look, I wasn't in the Navy, had no interest in it. Nevertheless, as I made my way along the coastline I saw that there were still stretches of untouched ocean that might be navigated. What put me off was spotting a ship out there - I have no idea how long it had been floating adrift, maybe even since all this first happened? I only know it was big, like a cruise ship or something - easy to see in spite of the fact it was quite far away. And it was going along nicely one minute, flowing through open waters - then the next it was being attacked by a patch of Rot that looked like it had moved towards it. Reminded me of the shark hunting its victims in *Jaws*. It was almost as if the Rot had a mind of its own; was the predator hunting the prey - and not just on a molecular level this time, but a visible one.

As I watched the ship being attacked, I gave another of those little shivers. Again, nothing to do with being cold - I had the SKIN, plus my other clothes, some of which I'd had to change because they'd begun to rot away; finding unaffected stuff was getting harder and harder as I went along... It was just the sight of that out there - enough to put me off trying to sail to better climes for a while at any rate.

My third bright idea? I made the pilgrimage down to our capital, and from there I would trace the train tracks to Folkestone and the Channel Tunnel entrance. Perhaps being so far under that water might have protected the tunnel itself, I thought. I encountered probably the most Rotten ever in that city, as you can probably imagine, and some were in the worst condition yet. People whose skin was dripping off them like so much melting wax, whose eyes were liquefying in what was left of their skulls. I found a large concentration at St Pancras, something inside them obviously mirroring my own need to get away from this island. All they would do was spread the infection - if it hadn't already drifted across by air or sea.

It got pretty hairy a few times during my time in that station, but I've learned not to let myself get surrounded by them - not to let myself get backed into corners, either, with no way out. These were much slower, which helped; easier to give them the slip. Not saying I didn't have to fight, because I did - this time with a pistol in one hand and my mace in the other - but invariably I won, like their hearts weren't in it anymore. I guess the longer the Rot had worked on them, the less they were even able to think about striking effectively... and yet they were all still doing it together. Still in those groups, still flocking - like the birds, like the horses.

There was an even worse sight waiting for me at the end of that line, however. The tunnel entrance, completely caved in - though there was Rotten water spilling out through gaps, having washed up bodies with it. These were covered in sludge and bilge, one piled upon another. It was a heartbreaking thing to see, mainly because I had no idea how many of these folk had still been 'okay' when it happened. Had they known, heard the cracking of the tunnel above them, tried to escape as the waves came crashing in through the ceiling?

I closed my eyes, the imagined horrors simply too much - even after everything I'd seen, everything I'd been through. Had to leave that place, once again not really knowing where I would go from there. Everything I thought of, every idea I had - after getting up when I'd been knocked down - none of it was working out. I was beginning to wonder if anything ever would, whether I'd just be doomed to walk amongst the Rotten, in this Rotting place forever.

I'm getting morbid again and I really don't mean to. Have no reason to at the moment. For the first time in as long as I can remember, there *is* actually hope. I'm *hopeful*. But there's a way to go before I can explain why, and it might take a few more of these entries before I can get you up to speed. For now, I think I'll call it a day. I've already been away too long, and if this experience has taught me anything it's that time is precious... it's rotting in its own way, too. Second by second, minute by minute.

I will be back, I promise. Then I'll tell you how it all started. Where that hope came from, and how it came into my life. Had some crap to go through first, but isn't that life whatever happens? You have to take the rough with the smooth, and often something that you think is the worst thing that's ever happened turns out to be the best. I know, I know... I'm keeping you in suspense, but I really do have to get back.

Dinner will be ready, you see, and she'll be waiting for me.

Shit... didn't mean to say that. Where's the erase on thi–

Stop.

CHAPTER NINE

Record:

Sometimes I'm my own worst enemy. You might have noticed that.

I'm also a sod for breaking my own rules, always have been and probably always will. I like to think I take precautions, but really I'm a spur of the moment kind of guy; I live on my wits, which is probably what made me so good at what I used to do. Probably what has kept me alive since the Rot took over, in spite of my own attempts to sabotage myself. Sometimes stuff like that ends up working for you, though, rather than against you.

I've found another quiet half hour, while people are sleeping. I'm far enough away that I don't think I'll wake them with my voice, and it's been nearly a week since my last entry so I think I'm probably overdue an update. Or to bring you *up* to date, if you see what I mean?

Right, well, as I continued to make my way in this world, I came to accept that nothing was ever going to change for the better, only get worse and worse. You can imagine what a frame of mind that puts someone in. I was in a bad way, let's just say that - probably even worse than those poor bastards out there who were losing pieces of themselves by degrees. Memories, personalities, fingers, toes... that kind of thing. I saw no evidence that this process was reversing itself, and with good reason, I later found out - nothing to support that nature was fighting back, that it had "found a way", as people used to say. Only that she seemed to have abandoned us, left us to our own sordid devices. And they were still quite sordid. Every now and again, regardless of the condition the Rotten might be in, I'd see them attempting to hump each other. Some had actually forgotten what they were supposed to do, what went where

– I'd see 'people' who were losing their shape attempting to thrust into what was left of ears or noses, usually just ragged holes. Either that or they didn't have the... equipment to do what it was they were trying to do. A nightmarish thing to witness, if you haven't already.

The Rotten were becoming more and more monstrous as time passed, even those who were still holding it off pretty well – and I hadn't come across anyone else on my travels who was immune, like Dennis, Carrie and Rakesh had been. Made me wonder if that had been the case at all? Perhaps I'd just assumed it, and if they hadn't been killed they might have ended up like all the rest of them. Maybe there had never been such a thing as immune – and, if so, was I the only one it hadn't touched, because of the SKIN? I couldn't attest to anywhere abroad, but it was certainly looking that way here, in this country.

Until I came across her.

As I think I mentioned in a previous recording, I don't get involved in other people's business, especially now; I keep myself to myself and leave the Rotten to it. That's how I'd live out my life, such as it was. But then it happened, a few miles outside one of the towns I was skirting, on my way back up the country after my disappointing – no, *downright disheartening* – trip to the capital and the tunnel. Once again, like so many things nowadays, I heard the trouble before I saw it. Screaming... a female voice. A woman's cries for help.

"Help me! Please... Oh please help!"

They carried in the silence of what had once probably been quite a picturesque part of the countryside, but was now covered in the telltale signs of the Rot. Withering foliage, turning brown and purple-grey; hedgerows that had folded over and were gasping their dying breaths. The noise was coming from a bridge not too far away. Made of stone that looked like it was just showing the first signs of the infection, it stoically maintained its original arched appearance.

Just off to the side, down the embankment a little way, I saw the woman who'd been yelling for attention – though where she thought that would come from out here, even before everything had gone haywire, was anyone's guess. She looked normal from this distance, no trace of the Rot on her face, nor down her neck – her hair was tied back in a pony-tail – and there was no rot on her shoulders or down her arms and legs; she was wearing some kind of vest-top and shorts, you see; had the whole Lara Croft thing going on. But just what was she doing out here in the first place? The same thing as me, avoiding the major population centres as best she could? *Maybe you could ask her, once you've given her a hand – once you've helped her,* I said to myself.

There were several Rotten surrounding her, all male, looking like they'd come from under the bridge – perhaps they'd gravitated to that place because they used to hang out there before 'the change'. Now it just looked like she'd encountered not one troll from out of a fairy tale, but a handful that were about to eat her up. "Oh God, please, someone help me!"

She was armed, but only with a knife it seemed – and this she swiped left and right in an arc, trying to ward off this group. Like that would do any good... Even if she stuck one of them, they probably wouldn't even feel it – the pain receptors in the brain are usually one of the first things to go, I'd worked out. I pursed my lips, watching as the pack drew nearer and nearer to her. Could I just sit there and wait for the inevitable to happen, especially if there was even the remotest chance she was okay, the first person I'd seen in all this time...? Surely the Rot would have affected her by now, if it was going to?

And if she was immune, was I about to watch one of the few chances humanity had left die right in front of my eyes – without doing a blessed thing about it?

Could I afford *not* to play the Good Samaritan this time? Could I just let the first glimmer of hope I'd had in a long while dwindle away?

You can probably guess the answer to that question. Before I had time to question my actions any further, I'd already set off and was making my way down the embankment to join in the party. By this time my guns had all gone the way of the dodo, as had the sword, axe and mace I'd picked up along the way. My weapon of choice at that particular time was a staff - using my rifle like one so many times had given me the idea. Made from the best bit of wood I was able to find and with sharpened ends, I'd actually become quite skilled with it - holding the Rotten at arm's length, dispatching them without having to go anywhere near. Mind you, for close-up combat, I'd taken a leaf out of Jane's book - no, don't mention Jane - and had a pair of lethal-looking scissors I'd swiped from a cottage the previous week tucked into my belt. I'd seen the damage a pair of those could do first hand, so...

I was hoping I wouldn't need them, though - and things went well, to begin with. The first Rotten, I stabbed in the back of the head with one end of the staff, hefting it like a spear, except I was keeping hold of it. The guy's skull was so soft it went in like a finger into an overripe tomato. A *rotten* tomato maybe that should be? The others were turning in my direction, which was what I wanted really - to take the focus away from Lara... in my head I'd already named her that, didn't matter what she turned out to be called. But as I brought up the staff to smack another in the face, she joined in, knifing a Rotten who'd turned his back on her.

Another came from my right, and I turned to do the same move again - staff up and striking squarely in what was left of the man's face. Only this time when I drove the wood forward, it snapped in two. The Rot has the worst timing ever when it comes to weaponry. Thinking fast, I turned each of the separate pieces of wood sideways, then rammed them into the chests of that man and one more who was attacking. One, when he dropped to the ground, broke up into goo, the body-slime oozing and seeping into the muddy grass.

That just left the last one to tackle, and my scissors were now out as he flung himself at me with a gurgle; all the language he could muster, with most of this mouth eaten away by the Rot. I thrust the sharp end of the scissors up into his stomach and he bent over, falling onto me – took all my balance to remain on my feet. Then I dragged the scissors upwards, opening his belly and chest, turning away as his innards splashed out over me and onto the ground beneath us.

Disgusted, I shoved the man off to join his fallen comrades on the field of conflict. It had been a while since I'd found myself in such an intensive fight – I'd forgotten how the adrenaline starts to pump, keeping you up until you're done. Bringing you crashing back down afterwards.

But nothing could have brought me crashing down to earth with a bump quicker than what happened next. I looked across at the woman, at Lara, and she offered a smile and a nod of thanks.

"Are you all right?" I asked her.

Another smile, another nod. Except there was something strange about both of these. The movements not quite right. Then I spotted the tiny traces of Rot at the corners of each eye, at her nostrils, like she'd been taking it as some sort of drug. Easily missed from the distance I'd first spotted her, it soon became apparent that she wasn't normal in the slightest. "Help... please help... oh God... please!" she screamed, even though I was only a couple of feet away. Now the appeal sounded very much like that holy man's, back at the shopping centre had, begging for his Lord to do something. For this woman, however, they were just words that had become stuck; an old fashioned CD skipping or an even older broken record repeating the same things over and over. Something she'd been saying when everything went pear-shaped – stuck in a frozen moment of time?

Then came the lunge, and she was close enough that I wasn't able to dodge it. Lara – the only name I would ever have for her now – tripped as she did so, the knife in her grasp plunging into my left thigh. It went through the material of my jeans – the cargos I'd originally snatched having long-since perished – and penetrated both the SKIN, and *my* skin.

I let out a furious cry, directed more at myself than at Lara for doing this – though there was a good deal of hate in it for her as well, don't get me wrong. Staggering back, I took the knife away with me, wrenching it out of her grasp and managing to knock her away with the back of my fist at the same time. The wound was agony and I transferred my weight to my good leg, hopping back out of her reach. But, like the other Rotten, Lara didn't know when to quit. They never do.

Once again, she charged – but this time I had the scissors held upright as she fell onto me. They went in at about where the liver is, as we both flopped over and onto the slushy ground. Lara kicked and writhed for a few minutes, but when her movements stopped I knew she was dead. That was when I heaved her off me and lay there, trying not to think about the throbbing at my thigh – trying not to think about the fact that the knife was the only thing sealing the gap in my SKIN. The blade might already be infected, in which case so was I – but if it wasn't, could I be quick enough to pull it out before the Rot ferreted its way in? I knew that the SKIN would knit itself together around the wound – it was one of the things Weeks had taught me that I had listened to. But I didn't know how long it would take, nor how much blood I'd lose in the process. If the SKIN healed itself over the cut in time, then it would start to reprocess any blood I was losing after that, even start to heal my wound. But could it get back what I might have lost in the meantime...? And that's even if the blade hadn't nicked an artery or something. I'd bleed out for sure at that point... though I suspected it had actually hit the pin in that leg, which was why it hadn't gone all the way in.

"Fuck!" I shouted, though there was nobody around to hear me. So much for the story of the Samaritan. What was that old phrase? No good deed goes unpunished? This one certainly hadn't.

Took me a while to summon up the courage to even look down at my leg, let alone do anything about it. The jeans material was wet, my blood seeping through no matter what I did. "Fuck!" I said again, almost a whisper this time. I gritted my teeth and went for broke, sitting up and grabbing the knife handle, then yanking out the blade.

I let out an almighty scream, not at all butch - more like a little girl wailing for her mother. No... that just makes me think of Jane again. Wish I could tell you that I handled it better, but it probably hurt as much as when I crashed that test plane; at least then they'd had me under within seconds of reaching me, and I didn't know a thing until I woke up in the hospital. This I *did* know about; this I felt. It took all my willpower not to just black out, like I had done after the chopper crash. I ripped off a piece of my coat sleeve and tied it around the thigh, in lieu of the SKIN reforming again - might even help it along, I figured. It would definitely stem the bleeding...

But then what? Nothing for miles in any direction that I could see - definitely nothing back where I'd come from. Nothing but rotting land. I cursed the fact that my staff was broken, because I could really have used it as a crutch. Instead, I had to try and get up that banking, crawling - felt like even the slope was working against me, the Rot gaining more and more ground the harder I tried. Got up to the top eventually, though. Managed to get to my feet, too. Walking would not be as easy, I soon realised, keeping weight off my wounded leg, favouring the other one. I fell over so many times just hobbling away from that bridge, from the scene of yet another trap the Rotten hadn't really planned, but which had worked a treat on this stupid sap.

I set off, carrying on along the 'path' I'd been walking when I heard those cries for help in the first place.

Should've just ignored them, I kept telling myself over and over. Should've, could've, would've... No excuses; got caught again - and I had always been taught to take responsibility for my own fuck-ups. That was when there *were* other people I could blame, of course; people other than the Rotten. Who, by the way, in my head had become a species in their own right, set apart from me, setting them apart from what they had been before all this happened. Now they were something else, something not even related to me anymore - not even remotely human. Something hideous, to be scorned. My enemy. Everything I stood - when I could stand - against. Pure emotion, the basest of instincts.

The hatred coursing through me gave me strength - and no, the irony wasn't wasted on me. But I like to think my mother's survival instinct had something to do with it again. Drove me on, hobbling and falling over so many times, only to pick myself back up again. If I sat down and gave in this time, that would be it. The end of me. No more feeling sorry for myself, I had to go on. Had to make it to somewhere.

Had to have hope in *something*.

By the time I crested that final hill, by the time I saw it ahead of me, I was virtually crawling again. On my hands and knees, though it was killing my injured thigh - then on my belly like a snake. There appeared to be an unaffected building ahead of me, another oasis in the middle of this brown desert the countryside had become. Somewhere that looked small and stable enough to hide in, to shut myself away from the Rotten until I'd recovered. To let the SKIN do its job.

I didn't realise as I made my way up that path what kind of structure it was, though there were signs of it everywhere - on the roof for one thing. But inside it couldn't be ignored. And so I struggled up the aisle, the red velvet carpet showing only the faintest hint of Rot. Crawled between those pews, heading for the steps at the front. The weak light of that day was pawing at the stained glass windows, which depicted saints and angels.

I made it to the steps and managed to touch the altar before I passed out, feeling like I'd achieved something – when in fact I'd achieved sod all once again. I'd reached a small chapel in the middle of nowhere. So what?

So *everything*, as I would discover the next time I came to.

Stop.

CHAPTER TEN

Record:

Have you ever been in love? I thought I was once or twice.

First time was at school and, looking back, it was probably just a crush. Didn't stop it hurting, though, when she fell in love with someone else. Second time was in my twenties and it hurt a whole hell of a lot more when it fell through. I thought we were on the same page; she messed me about... didn't end well. Other than that, as I think I've said, women have come and gone in my life. Love was for other people, didn't think it would ever happen for me - and especially after the apocalypse hit. Just shows you how wrong you can be.

Because when I woke up in that chapel, her face was the only thing I could see - and I think I knew it... *felt* it there and then, or maybe that's me projecting things onto the past that weren't there. Didn't say anything at the time, mainly because she was holding a crossbow levelled at my head; one of those new-fashioned repeaters, judging from the cartridge underneath.

Not the best of starts, I'll grant you - but she warmed to me.

"Easy," she said as I turned and started to sit up. "Take it nice and slow."

"I... I don't think I can take it any other way," I assured her, which was the truth. I felt like I'd gone ten rounds with a heavyweight boxer - but then blood-loss will do that to you. The SKIN would replenish my reserves eventually, but how long had I been unconscious? There was only one way to find out - and my mind immediately flashed back to *The*

White Hart's cellar, where I'd asked exactly the same question.

"I have no idea," was the answer this woman gave me. "I just found you here... I've been gone nearly a day." Her raven hair was in a bob, eyes so big and round they took up most of her face - overwhelming those other delicate features. She was dressed not that dissimilarly to the guards at the facility, a kind of tracksuit or jumpsuit, but with a jacket over the top. A strap ran over her left shoulder, down through the valley of her breasts, and round past her right hip - holding up some kind of messenger bag that was dangling down behind her. The whole outfit was topped off with a pair of leather boots that came to her knees and were covered in mud and slime.

"Gone?" I asked, shaking my head. I wasn't fazed by the fact she was talking to me, making sense. But I *was* looking for signs of the Rot on her face and hands, not that they were always evident there; could have been under her clothes for all I knew, right the way up her back. Could turn any second and just shoot me in the head. Even now, those parts of the brain that made her *her* might be getting eaten way.

"Yes," she said curtly, still training the bolt on me. "I needed some supplies."

I looked around, wondering if I'd been taken somewhere - but no, I was still in the chapel, still surrounded by the saints and the angels. "You... you *live* here?"

She frowned at me as though that was on odd thing to ask, then *she* asked: "What kind of polymer is that?"

"Come again?"

"The webbing, your protective suit. Does it incorporate nanites?" Now she was frowning because she was studying the SKIN. She cocked her head and I waited for the change to come over her; for the woman to start screaming or laughing or... She just righted her head again, and said:

"I've never seen anything like it in my life. I'm assuming it covers the whole of your body?"

I just nodded. Didn't know what else to do.

"But it's damaged, right?" She pointed to my thigh with the crossbow and I followed her gaze, the first time I'd thought about the injury since I woke up. Wasn't hurting anymore at least, so there was that. The material from my sleeve I'd tied around it was still there, so I couldn't see whether the SKIN was healed or not. I made to remove the bandage and the woman took a step closer, bringing the crossbow up to her shoulder - ensuring I knew she meant business.

"I said easy," she snapped.

"I was just going to... Look, *you* were the one who asked."

She thought about this for a second and nodded. "Go on."

I unwrapped the dressing, pulling aside the torn edges of my jeans. The SKIN beneath it had indeed knitted itself back together again. The skin beneath that was on its way to doing the same, but would leave a nasty scar behind. "Fixed," I said simply, as the woman seemed to respond better to the more direct approach.

"What happened?" she said then.

"What do you think? I got attacked," I informed her. "Actually, I was trying to help this woman who I thought—"

"Did you get *infected*?" That was rich, coming from someone who was standing there with no protection whatsoever. Who might be covered in Rot from the neck down for all I knew. But she was waiting for a reply, demanding it without even saying a word. She does that... Can say something to you without even having to open her mouth; could just be how she is or it might be how we've come to feel about each...

Shit, jumping ahead again. Sorry.

I was going to answer that I didn't know, because I didn't. I felt fine, but I'm sure most people do before that change comes on them. Just as this woman might turn at any moment, who was to say I wouldn't instead? I was pretty sure the SKIN would have detected something by now, though - set off some sort of system-wide alert. Confident enough to shake my head in answer to her question, anyway. "What about you?"

She just stared at me. "Does it look like I'm infected to you?"

I shrugged.

This isn't painting a very good picture of her, I know, but I'm telling the story warts and all. We didn't really know each other, were definitely suspicious of one another. And still, given all that, I felt an undeniable attraction.

"Well, I'm not."

"You'll forgive me if I don't take your word for it," I said. "I've seen people who looked okay, only for them to go nuts in seconds. The lady I was trying to save back there, she looked fine, but when I got to her..."

The woman in front of me held up her hand. "Okay, okay. Point taken. But I haven't got the disease, trust me. I've done tests and everything. I... well, I'm immune."

"Right." I said it slowly, without a hint of trust - or sarcasm, though that's what she heard in my voice.

"You either believe me or you don't."

"I'd believe it a whole lot more if I could see the rest of you."

She shook her head. "Not gonna happen."

I think I cracked a smile then and said something stupid like, "Can't blame a guy for trying, though." What a charmer, eh?

But in spite of herself, she smiled back – the crossbow lowering a little. "Here, let me show you something," she said, then saw me smile again. "Not that."

The woman motioned for me to get up, which was a lot harder than it sounded. I was still pretty wobbly, and needed to hang on to the altar to begin with. When I took my first few steps I felt like a toddler again, or doing my physio after the accident, my pinned leg still weak and healing. Just like I had on my way there, I stumbled, about to fall over – but then suddenly she was beside me, holding me upright, putting my arm around her shoulders. Carrying me.

"De…Decided I'm not dangerous after all, then," I said.

"Jury's still out," she told me. "But in your condition I figure you're not really up to pulling anything."

As she took me through to the back of the chapel, I looked about me again, looked up. "What?" she asked.

"Aren't you frightened of all this coming down on your head?"

She gave a little laugh. "Not really."

"I've seen the Rot do it to bigger places. You must have seen it as well."

"Is that what you're calling it: the Rot?"

"How else would you describe it?"

It was her turn to shrug. "Those people out there, the buildings and everything else… they're not rotting in the conventional sense of the word."

"Okay." Again, I said it slowly and with very little conviction.

"Here," she said as she opened the door and took me

into a back room, which must have belonged to whatever vicar had tended to this parish; a private space, with books on shelves and a table in the middle of the room, with what looked weed killer sprayers stacked against the wall to our left, and against the right, a camp bed. On the table were a couple of microscopes like the ones I'd been using back at St August's, one rigged up to a large battery on the floor. There were test-tubes as well in wooden holders, glass beakers with liquid in them. It looked like a massive version of a kid's chemistry set. She flipped a switch on one of the microscopes, pointed to the lens.

"I've seen all this before," I told her.

"Just look," she prompted.

So I did. There was a sample under there already, at quite a high magnification. "It's stone," she told me. "The same stone this place is made from."

The Rot was attacking it, just like I'd seen before. "I don't see what..."

"Keep watching," she said and I did, as something was introduced to the sample - a yellowish fluid. Almost immediately, the Rot stopped; not only that, the parts of the sample that I'd seen being eaten away were beginning to be restored to their normal state.

"What the..." I looked up and saw she was standing next to me, holding a pipette.

"I treated the whole place with it, inside and out," she informed me, smiling even more broadly and pointing to the spraying equipment - which I now noticed included what looked like a huge industrial hypodermic needle made out of metal. "As best I could anyway. First thing I did when I had enough; I needed somewhere safe to continue my work."

"But what... I don't understand."

Again, I'll admit that a lot of what she said next went

over my head. Head hurting time, actually; eyes glazing over. Something to do with developing the treatment from her blood, from the proteins? I do remember she said something along the lines of: "Same theory as introducing an antagonistic organism to reduce the ability of fungus to colonise wood in dry rot. Only effective if you catch it early enough, though. Works on stone and wood, obviously... Paper." She waved her hand over the books. "Food." Now she took out an apple from her bag - the freshest apple I'd ever seen in fact - and she bit into it with a crunch. "Tastes a bit weird, but better than what I was living off before... Then again, I don't suppose you've had that problem, have you?" She touched my face and I flinched, not expecting it. "I'm sorry, it's just I've never... *Where* did you get it?"

"Long story," was all I'd say at that time.

"I assume it's what's been keeping you alive all these months, that tech?"

"Not just the tech. I've kept *myself* alive," I argued.

"Of course... Well, the 'Rot' as you call it, that's been doing the same for those people out there, keeping them alive. You ever see any of *them* eat?"

"I..." Now I thought about it, I hadn't. I guess I just assumed they ate rotting food, drank stale water - what harm could it do them, after all? But then I thought about Mum, about her refusal to eat - about how she'd even forgotten *how* to eat.

"What do you mean, keeping them alive? They're all dying."

"They're *changing,*" she corrected me, as if to reinforce what she'd said earlier about the disease we were facing. "Just like the environment is, to accommodate all this. Look, when we die, we become little more than necrotic tissue - it's true." I'm paraphrasing here, so stick with me... "But those people out there are still very much alive. It's all part and parcel of the same thing, everything's balancing out and it'll keep doing that until—"

"It's taken over," I butted in. I was still thinking about it as the enemy, as an invading force. Wasn't how she regarded it at all.

"Fascinating really, when you think about it."

"It's *terrifying*," I said, correcting her this time, but she said nothing in return. "How do you know so much about it? Were you responsible for it or something?" And I imagined her then, sitting in some lab somewhere, a place like the facility - working on the Rot, maybe even as a weapon like Dennis had suggested.

She laughed again. "I *wish!*" Then realised what she'd said and shook her head. "Let me rephrase that, I wish I was clever enough to come up with something like that. You'd have to be a genius." From where I was standing, she didn't seem too damned shabby in that department. A better mind than mine... "No, I've just had a long time to study it, that's all. In fact that's the only thing I've been doing all this time, apart from surviving, like yourself. Helped me to come up with my little cocktail, stop the spread of the disease in this place. And I bet you thought it was some kind of divine intervention protecting it, right?" She shook her head. I found out later that she had no interest in religion; was an atheist, in fact. Divine intervention hadn't helped that priest back in the shopping centre, why should it have helped this place?

I ignored that comment anyway. "So this *is* a disease then?"

"Any disturbance of the function or structure of a body... or object, is a disease." It was just a confirmation of what I'd thought myself, my amateur studies - which were like child's play compared with what she'd been doing. I'd been the one with the kid's chemistry set, if anything.

"Any idea how it came about?"

She shook her head again. "Not yet, but I'm working on

that, too."

"So, what, you're some kind of doctor, scientist...?"

"Biochemist... at least that's what one of my doctorates is in."

"One? Christ!" I said and she pulled a face, wagged her finger.

"Remember where you are." Then she laughed once more and I couldn't help joining in a little. "Yeah, afraid so. I was one of those girls who was busy studying when the others were off chasing boys - probably boys like you." I blushed at that, but couldn't help thinking it was some kind of veiled insult about my wasted youth. "Hit uni early, promising career in the private sector, no husband, no kids or pets... yada, yada, yada... End of the world, I'm immune. Whaddya gonna do?"

"But... but you've come up with the *cure*," I said. "It doesn't have to be the end."

Her face soured. "It's still in its early stages, and although I've tested it on organic matter, I still haven't tested it on human tissue. That's my next step in these little clinical trials."

I nodded, then suddenly thought...

"Look, we've been talking here and I don't even know your name."

For a moment it looked like she wasn't going to tell me, then she blurted out, "Kim... It's Kim Bedford."

"Keller. Adam Keller."

We didn't shake hands or anything quite as formal at that, because the trust still wasn't there really, but Kim was interested enough to say next: "So, what's your story?"

I grinned. "Well, you know, it's funny you should ask that..."

Pause.

Resume recording:

I played her my journal - again, warts and all - so she'd get a pretty clear sense of who I was. Thought it would be better than just recounting everything again, editing selected bits. Thought it would make her trust me more... although she still sat with the crossbow within reach.

Kim had me pause a few times, so she could make herself drinks; once a coffee, a couple of times tea - both with the special ingredient she'd shown me through the microscope. It has a kind of brackish flavour, that stuff, but you get used to it - like she said, it was better than doing without. I sometimes think it was more of a habit than anything else, a routine carried over from before the change - like she was sitting and listening to some sort of radio drama with a cuppa. Unfortunately, this drama had been all too real and Kim knew that - I hadn't made any of this up and she could see I hadn't. For one thing I had tears in my eyes at certain points.

By the time it drew to a close, Kim did too.

The crossbow forgotten about, she stood and walked over to me and gave me the biggest hug I've ever had from anyone in my life - including from Mum. And I hugged her back, the first proper human contact - if you could even call it that through the SKIN - I'd had in a long, long time. The first real human connection, as well, not just a one night stand like the one I'd been contemplating with that nurse so long ago back at the facility, but something that meant so much more. Two survivors, clinging to each other in a crazy topsy-turvy world.

I wonder sometimes if it was that moment I fell in love with her, but no - it was definitely before. Feels sometimes like I've always loved Kim, which I know is the kind of soppy thing people say who're in the middle of it. She might even tell you that it's a disease too in its own way, because it alters the brain's chemistry. If so, then I'm happy to have caught it.

Kim told me a little about her life beyond the basics after she'd heard about mine. Mother and father had both died quite early on in her life, much earlier than mine and at the same time, in a car crash, leaving her to be brought up by her aunt. She'd won various scholarships, so money hadn't really been a problem, but it had been a lonely existence for her even before all this had happened. In fact, it had taken her a few days to even notice what was happening in the sleepy village where she'd set up home not that far from here. They say that the cleverest people often feel the most isolated, and Kim was the living, breathing proof of that. I can't ever say that I'm on her level intellectually – I thought I was doing okay until I met her – but we do have a hell of a lot in common besides that. Taste in books, in films and music...

But I'm getting off track again. What happened next? Well, once we'd both rested up and talked some more – talked for hours and hours and it still didn't seem enough – I was drafted in to help with the next stage of the plan to rescue humanity and this planet.

"We're going to need a human test subject," she informed me. "I've been putting it off for a while now, just because I wasn't sure whether I'd be able to manage it on my own." She didn't need to tell me how hard it was to try and capture one of the Rotten.

But, unlike me, Kim had it all plotted out. Some of her happiest memories growing up were when she and her father used to go out fishing and hunting. "He was a real live off the land kind of bloke," she told me, and when she spoke about him I could see the love in her eyes, how much she missed him still. "Most effective trap for our kind of prey, without causing too much injury, is a snare trap." You've probably seen these yourself, where a noose is hidden on the floor. As soon as an animal steps on it and the trigger is released, they go flying into the air to hang there.

We wouldn't be using trees for our 'engine', though - instead Kim had already chosen a location to set the trap; had already treated the building, in fact. A small single-screen cinema she knew well, one of those places showing classics that she'd caught before the Rot had set in too badly.

The hardest part would be getting close enough without drawing attention to set the trap, but then she'd done her homework in that department as well. Watching patterns of Rotten traffic; how many people were usually in one place at any given time, including inside the cinema. She'd worked out that first thing in the morning it was relatively quiet; probably because the cinema used to be closed at that time. Easy enough to head in, set up the trap, then retreat again.

Kim had done a great job designing the trap itself, so good her dad would have been proud, I think. So, during one of those quieter periods we set to work. This involved running a rope over the length of the cinema awning - which stated that the last thing to be shown there had been Disney's *Pinocchio*. Attached to it was a sack full of stones as counterbalance - everything treated so they wouldn't just fall apart on us. We hauled this up together, using the awning as an anchor, then set the metal spring trigger, driven into the ground. There were a couple of unwanted visitors, but Kim soon dealt with those using the crossbow - headshots, as it was the only sure-fire way of shutting them up quickly enough.

Then we just had to wait...

Over the course of a week or more, we kept returning during those lulls to see what we'd bagged, Kim rejecting any specimens that were too far gone. At some point in the future we might be able to bring them back from the brink, but it was highly unlikely, Kim said. We decided to do them the favour of putting them out of their misery.

Neither of us was expecting what happened that last time. A boy was in the trap, probably no more than about ten years of age, with tufts of ginger hair, wearing only a pair of faded and ripped jeans. The closer we came to inspect him, the more perfect he seemed for Kim's purposes. It wasn't until we were there, trying to subdue him and get him down - get him away from that place as soon as possible - that he started to scream. Kim used another of her concoctions - a bit like chloroform, she told me - to try and knock him out, covering the boy's mouth with a cloth, but it wasn't doing much good... not at first, anyway. Perhaps it was the Rot protecting him from those chemicals, just like the SKIN would have done with me. And by the time it started to have an effect, it was already too late.

There weren't supposed to be that many Rotten around, and yet this time there suddenly were, as if they'd worked out what we'd been trying to do. Or the Rot had. There were loads, beginning with a man and woman who rushed out of the cinema's foyer, then rushed *us*. I only got a glimpse of them as they sprang towards us, rags of clothing flying at their back like speed lines in a cartoon. The woman's face had completely fallen away down one side, like so much putty, while the man's body was doing a similar thing - shoulders slanted, his gait causing him to lope. I had no idea whether these were the kid's parents or not - probably not, because the parental instinct didn't seem to be there with the Rotten; just look at what had happened at Jane's school - but it made no difference anyway.

I tugged on Kim's sleeve, and we switched places - so she could fire at the couple and I could handle the kid. He was still fighting us off, so in the end I punched him - not scientifically correct, I know, but we were against the clock. Several of Kim's bolts found a home in the torsos of the Rotten man and woman, but didn't bring them down. What's more, I could see dozens of figures bringing up the rear, flooding out of the showroom and into the foyer; we should have checked inside, but we had just assumed... Sloppy, very sloppy. I turned, hefting the kid onto my shoulder - then saw more of the Rotten behind us, appearing out of nowhere and confirming that this had to be an ambush.

"Shit... Kim, we have to move!"

She nodded and reloaded the crossbow with another cartridge, just as one Rotten woman came out of nowhere to shoulder her over and knock the weapon out of her hands. *"Kim!"*

From the floor, she waved a hand at me - for me to go. But none of this would be of any use if Kim didn't make it out. Besides, I was at the point by then that I *couldn't* leave her, no matter what she wanted. I stooped and grabbed the crossbow - firing indiscriminately left and right, clearing the way for her to get to her feet. Then clearing the path ahead of us to escape.

The crossbow clicked on empty and I threw it back over my shoulder, satisfied to see it tangle up in one of the Rotten's legs and trip them. The noise they were making was beyond anything I'd heard before, more throaty and gurgling, as if their larynxes were severely damaged - but the sounds were finding another way out somehow. Kim slipped and almost fell again, but I turned and kicked back at the figure grabbing her legs.

We turned a corner and... there was our escape: the Volvo Kim had treated so it would continue to run. It was how she made her way back and forth for supplies, and we'd parked it a short distance from the trap's site in case we needed it. Boy did we need it then, with so many of the Rotten gathering together and trailing us. Kim opened the back door and I threw the boy in, then we both clambered inside - Kim wise enough to trust me with the driving this time. I gunned the engine and put it in reverse, delighted to have a vehicle that *I* could rely on at last. We slammed back into a group of the Rotten, knocking them over, and by turns those around them as well - just like the pylons I'd seen in the field that time; human dominoes... well, not quite human, as some of these splattered on impact with the floor; virtually exploding, such was the advanced stage of Rot they were in.

I drove off in the other direction, both of us fighting for breath - then looking back; Kim over the seat, and me through the rear view. Both silently giving thanks that we'd been able to find someone who wasn't that far down the line already.

Someone we might be able to help, at last.

Stop.

CHAPTER ELEVEN

Record:

The results were amazing, I have to say.

Kim and I tied the boy up to a pair of wall-mounted candle holders at the back of the chapel. It was the only place where we could keep him secure and also administer the serum properly, as Kim needed easy access to his veins. But when we stepped back we both realised what it looked like, his arms out to each side like that.

"Not superstitious, are you?" she asked me.

"Well, *he* came back from the dead - maybe we can do the same for this poor kid."

"Make him a real boy again, eh?" She smiled and I nodded.

Leaving him there for the time being, we went into the back room - Kim to have a well deserved drink... of tea again, that was. She'd told me about a bottle of scotch she'd found and treated, but she was saving that for a really special occasion. Maybe when the boy showed signs that he might recover from the Rot, which we'd discovered was already attacking his feet and lower legs when we did an examination.

I don't know what it was, maybe the closeness to death we'd both encountered back there - although we'd both faced that a few times separately - but we eventually found ourselves sitting together on the camp bed that Kim had been using to sleep on; I'd claimed one of the pews out in the main body of the chapel for that. The camp bed reminded me a lot of the one inside my room at the facility, but I wasn't thinking about that back then. I was thinking more about Kim's hands touching my face again. My first thought was that she was examining the SKIN, feeling its texture - she'd been talking about a detailed study of the thing for a while.

But it was more than that; much more. Kim suddenly kissed me, and it felt... strange, artificial. "Can you feel that?" she asked me.

I half-nodded, half-shrugged. It was difficult to explain. Her hand reached down, into the pair of treated trousers she'd dug out for me not long after we met...

I can't believe I'm even saying all this. Can't believe I'm going into detail about what happened that night, especially now there's definitely a chance someone will listen to it.

I should stop there. But, well, I don't want to. It's the most fantastic thing that's ever happened to me and I just... Maybe I'll just play it for Kim and then wipe it. I dunno...

Let's just say that when Kim touched me there, things happened - but it wasn't the same, not through the SKIN. For the first time since I'd put it on, since the change happened, I truly hated the thing. Especially when Kim stood up in front of me and took her clothes off.

"You can check me now... if you want," she said.

I reached a trembling hand up and cupped a breast - one of those oh-so-perfect breasts of hers. And I could feel it, the weight of it, the smoothness... sort of. But I couldn't really *feel* it. My hand dropped and I looked away.

She looked hurt when I returned my gaze to her face. "What's the matter, don't you want to?"

That was just the thing, I wanted to so, so much. *Too* much. I couldn't explain it to her, but I didn't want our first time to be like this. "I..."

"It doesn't matter you know," she said. "We can still... do things. And if the serum works on the boy..."

She didn't, couldn't understand. Kim was immune, she'd be able to feel everything – and here was I stuck inside this giant bloody frogman's outfit. I'm sorry, but that's exactly what it felt like.

I got up, couldn't take it anymore. Couldn't take seeing her like that when there was nothing I could do about it. I rushed past her and into the chapel again, shaking my head.

As I looked to the side, I happened to see the boy's feet. Already, the Rot was clearing up; on the run from Kim's "antagonistic organism," as she'd called it, just like it had been in the building that surrounded us and kept us safe. I walked over, bending and taking another look. Yes, it was definitely improving – the battle being won. And hadn't Kim said that not only would it reverse the damage in cases like these, it could also protect against the disease in others?

Could protect me against it...

I looked around, saw where Kim had left the needles full of serum – one empty, another quite full. Without even stopping to think, without waiting for the boy to wake up – he could have been completely braindead for all I knew – I grabbed the needle and searched my arm for a vein.

"No!" I heard Kim scream from the doorway, covered up in a robe I'd never seen her wear before. It was satin, clinging to every inch of her, and did little to dissuade me. Then the needle was in, pushing through SKIN and skin alike, and I was pumping the yellow liquid into myself.

Kim paused, seeing that it was already too late. "How... how do you feel?" she asked me.

I didn't feel any different, to be honest – but then it was immunising me against the Rot, not reversing anything. Saying nothing, I walked back over to her and took her hand, took her back to the room beyond the chapel.

Smiling, I undid her robe and then pushed it back over her shoulders until she was naked again. Next I took off my own clothes.

And then, in spite of Kim's protests, I shed my SKIN.

We made love on that camp bed, not just once but many times that night. Like I say, it was the most wonderful night of my entire life, being that intimate with someone. With Kim.

When we were finished and she was lying there in my arms, I heard her give a little laugh. I thought I'd done something wrong, hadn't been good enough to satisfy this wonderful, perfect woman. But it wasn't that.

"You want to know a secret?" she asked.

"I don't know," I said, suddenly very worried, "do I?"

"My middle name..." Kim continued.

"What about it?"

"It's Evelyn, after my mum."

Took a second for the penny to drop and then I laughed myself. "Adam and... You're joking?"

She laughed again, took my hand and kissed it, then she sat up on her elbow and kissed my mouth softly once more.

SKIN; without the SKIN. There was simply no comparison.

Pause.

Resume record:

So, there you have it – the night we finally got together.

There have been a lot more nights since, but no need to harp on about all that. You want to know about the boy, I'm sure. The one we adopted in the end. Well, I said at the start of this particular recording that the results were amazing, and they definitely were. The Rot was beaten back in him, disappearing from his body completely –

although Kim would continue to test blood samples to make sure things were progressing as they should. We were both tested, in fact, Danny and myself... Oh, Danny is what we called him; he couldn't remember his actual name, probably something to do with the transition back, Kim explained.

"His memory might return in time, or it might not. The brain's a complicated thing, Adam."

I'll never forget his screaming though when he woke up in the chapel, not the cries of a Rotten this time but that of a scared lad not knowing where... or who he was.

"Help... Please help..." we heard, and came rushing out. I was reminded a little of Lara and the bridge, because she'd said exactly the same thing and then still turned out to be infected. Danny wasn't though, that much was apparent by the questions he began asking as soon as he saw us.

"What's happened to me? Why am I tied up like this? Are you going to kill me?" Poor little guy.

We explained as best we could, but I'm not sure he got it all the first time - it's a lot to process and for him it must have been a bit like waking up from a coma. It's gradually sunk in; he couldn't really deny it when he saw what had happened to the countryside around here. When he saw his first Rotten on supply runs with myself and Kim.

"You mean... *I* was like them?" he spluttered. Takes some getting used to, I guess.

"But it means we can probably help the others... a lot of them anyway," Kim said to Danny.

Oh, by the way, we named him after Dad: Daniel William Keller. Seemed as good a name as any until his own came back to him. Was it wrong that I hoped a little that it didn't, that none of his past came back? Because even if that couple at the cinema had nothing to do with him, chances are his own folks were either turned or dead. Besides, we were getting used to him being 'ours' by then. We'd have family dinners - still do - where we'd chat and laugh and just do the things that families do. It was something I don't think either of us, Kim or me, thought we'd ever have.

And we made plans, Kim talking about refining the serum and how to distribute it. I suggested finding a serviceable plane and treating that, then flying over a town or city and spraying the formula - like crop dusting. That was okay as far as tests were concerned, but Kim broached another idea, something a bit more drastic: creating another ground zero effect.

"You mean like a bomb?" I said.

"Something that would scatter a concentrated version of the serum over a wider area, which should then spread."

"Like the Rot did in the first place," I said, rubbing my bristled chin. Have I mentioned how nice it was just to grow hair again, and to be able to *feel* that hair. Not that I wasn't grateful for the SKIN - which Kim is still running tests on by the way, having detached the recording device for me to carry on using... obviously.

Not sure I'll need it much longer though, because we're almost ready. Ready at least to try. And if we can pull it off, then...

Just one more thing to report before that happens. Kim's pregnant. Yeah, I know... When she started being sick all the time, I immediately jumped to the wrong conclusion - thinking negatively again, that everything was going so right something had to go wrong eventually. But it wasn't the Rot, she just had morning sickness... which, for the record, is a complete misnomer. She was sick morning, noon, and night.

Danny's been brilliant, I have to say. He's very much looking forward to a little baby brother or sister.

I look back on those first recordings now and shudder. Things have gradually turned around for me, and that's what we're hoping to do for the world. I'll let you know how it all goes, don't worry, though I'm fully expecting you to see for yourself. To be making recordings of your own before too long.

Kim can't really drink that whisky now, in her condition, so it's left to me to toast the future. Well, here's mud in your eye...

Ugh, tastes like fucking mud as well! Remind me never to drink treated whisky ever again.

End Recording.

CHAPTER TWELVE

Record:

I... I know what you're expecting to hear now, but you'd be wrong.

Been a while since I've had the heart to pick this damned thing up and speak into it. Not... not sure I'm ready even now, but...

Not enough mud-whisky in the world.

I... no, sorry. Not yet... I can't talk about it yet.

Stop.

Record:

Shit.

Look, what do you want from me? Okay, they're dead... Both dead.

Fuck... I thought I was prepared for this, it's been a long time, but... hold on... Can't seem to stop crying. Wait, I think I've... yeah... So, that was cutting a long story short, wasn't it? Kim and Danny, both dead – them and... Oh God, my baby... my little...

Would... would have been my first born.

You want to know how, though, don't you? Fuck, I don't know if I can even... Everything was going to be so great, everything was going to be good again. There was hope again.

It happened while I was out on a run, scrounging up more supplies for the bomb we'd been building. We were almost there, as I think I told you when I last picked up the recorder, just a few more parts and—

As soon as I opened the door to the chapel and called out to Kim and Danny, I knew something was wrong. I'd found a working shotgun during one of the excursions, which we'd treated, and it was this I raised when there was no reply from either of them. Then I saw the altar had been knocked over, and one of the stained glass windows was smashed.

"Kim!" I shouted again. "Danny..."

I made my way through into the back room, saw the scratches on the wood of the door. The Rotten, had to be - they'd got in! Kim had another crossbow by this time, but if there were too many of them... I shook away the thought, reminded myself what a good fighter she was, how long she'd survived for until I crashed into her life.

I toed open the door, saw broken glass and wood on the floor, books scattered about. Swallowing dryly, I stepped through and...

Saw Danny, standing and looking down, sobbing. Kim was by his feet, covered in blood. She was looking up at me, but I could tell there was nothing of her in those huge, lifeless, glassy eyes. The crossbow was in her hand, but she'd obviously not been able to stop her attacker.

"Oh... oh no," I whimpered. "Danny... Danny, what happened?"

It was only then that the boy turned towards me, still crying - except the expression on his face wasn't one of remorse. He was grinning from ear to ear like a loon, foamy saliva dripping from his mouth. I looked down and saw the piece of glass in his hand, either from one of the beakers or the window behind me, it didn't matter - all that mattered was what he'd done with it. What he'd been *forced* to do by the fucking Rot.

Because his neck was covered in the stuff, like he was wearing a scarf - tracking up one side of his face to his hairline, into one of his eyes and sending it blind, though it was still shedding tears like the other one.

"Danny... no," I breathed.

His grin became a snarl and, still sobbing, he began towards me. I backed away at first, retreating into the chapel – and then into one of the pews, my old bed, which I fell over. Danny followed me, letting out the most tremendous wail. I couldn't get my head around the fact that this was the boy we'd had breakfast with that morning. Worse even than when we'd first found him, the Rot racing through the kid now.

I scrambled to my feet, shotgun up again and pointing at him. "Stop... please Danny. I don't want to..." But part of me did, God help me! Part of me wanted to blow his head clean off for what he'd done. I had to keep reminding myself that it wasn't him, it was our old enemy returned. It had somehow found a way to defeat our...Kim's serum, to take back what we'd stolen from it.

Danny paused, cocking his head. Maybe some part of him recognised me, or understood what I was saying – understood what had happened here. Because his brow furrowed, and I swear the tears that came next were genuine. Just before he took that piece of glass and tore into his own face, raking down the side of it like he was trying to cut away the Rot, ending with a flourish across his throat, blood jetting out across the chapel floor.

Then came the rumbling sound, the crack in that floor. The cracks up the walls of the chapel – which caused a section of the roof to cave in where Danny was standing. I didn't see anything else for the dust, just got out through the front doors again, watching as the main part of the chapel collapsed, like St August's had done so long ago.

I stood there for a few moments, then dropped to my knees – as I had that day as well. I'd lost so much more this time, though. And I still had the shotgun in my hand. Even put the barrel in my mouth, placed my finger on the trigger.

But I knew what would happen if I pulled it. Knew that it would probably just click uselessly, knowing my luck, deny me my end; the serum failing. Eventually, I threw it aside and burst into tears, not even testing that theory.

Took me all my strength to pull back from that one. But I'm a survivor, like Mum was... Like Kim was.

I'm a survivor, and this is what happened next.

Stop.

Record:

Sorry, I needed to get myself together properly to tell you about afterwards.

It wasn't just a survival instinct that got me going, it was also a craving for revenge. I'd finish up the bomb, detonate it and—

Didn't take me long to realise that wasn't going to happen. Even if I exploded it, the serum clearly didn't work - or didn't work *permanently*. I don't know whether it was just that something was wrong with Kim's formula, or whether she wasn't really immune at all - perhaps it had got to her in the end as well, I have no way of knowing. Hell, maybe *I'd* given it to her? Not even going to go there again, because I'll find some way of ending myself without the need of a shotgun - and I have to carry on.

Didn't matter, it was pointless. Ground zero would only buy some time, but then what? Without Kim, there was no way of refining the treatment; she was the brains... the brains behind all this. Had been the true Godsend. Kim, my love.

But the injection would buy *me* some time, to maybe find someone else who could continue her work. At least find somewhere that might be unaffected. I picked my way through the rubble of the church, but everything was pretty much destroyed. I stopped when I started to see limbs in there, but by that time the Rot had taken hold of the site anyway.

Luckily, there were still some stocks of serum in the Volvo – we'd placed spray-packs in the boot in case of emergencies. And the car was still working... for now. So, I'd revert to my previous plan – but instead of crop dusting, I'd begin my search.

I found a plane I could use and treated it, which would keep it going for a while. My travels had taken me the length and breadth of this country, so I'd make the hop abroad and begin there.

And that's what I've been doing ever since...

By air at first – damn, I miss flying – then by land, by whatever transport I could find, I searched and searched. When my stocks of serum ran out, I attached what was left of the SKIN – one of the few things that *had* survived the chapel – to the hull of a boat and navigated waters I once swore I would never attempt. I've survived, and I've seen sights you could not possibly believe.

Rivers of melting people, flowing into each other because of the Rot. Snow and ice infected with the stuff, turning from white, from clear, to brown and purple-grey. Mountains cracking up the middle, split in two and tumbling to the ground. Whole cities the size of which we could not even imagine at home, flattened, having succumbed to the Rot, before sinking into a massive crater in the ground.

I might have taken more days than Fogg did, but I made it around the world all right, just like I did when I was backpacking; as the skies above me turned from blue with fluffy clouds to drab and bleak, mirroring the Earth itself. I gave up trying to find a cure and instead focussed solely on my secondary objective, spurred on by stories told by those who were still able to speak, even if they could do little else – the Rot having left their minds last after ravaging their bodies. They spoke of somewhere sacred, a tiny part of this globe that the Rot hadn't been able to 'change'. Maybe it was just a myth, just hope, but I had to know for sure...

I...

Stop:

Record:

And now I'm coming to the... edge... no, to the *end* of all this; coming to the end in more ways than...

Foot...*found* the first signs of it on me earlier this water...*week*. Might have been with me from the start, or might have been down to the muck I've been farm...*forced* to living off - which, come think... *to* think of it I ran through in... ran out of later...*long* ago. Can't remember who...*when*. The Rot has been take me piece by...spreading that me, eating away me...

But must case... *carry* on. Need to... there is still house...*hope*. You know what, it might be the...the Dad... *disease* talking to me, but realised something. We were rotting long before it came along. Us, people...the plug... the *planet*... what we'd done to the gift we'd been given... Might bo... bo...*be* better now... keeping me alive... *fuck!*

NO! There... I see it. I can... Green, I green see. Right there, can't yet...*you*...?

Trees, flowers... a cool, clear road...*river*... An... an Eden.

Home... *hope*.

Trying to... to get there, it's not eend...*easy*... my legs... they... Need to... It's so, so beautiful... Can... can you hope...*hear* me...? Is this still re...r'cording... Ha ha... cording... I think, I think I lost the corder back in... Did I ever have...? My aren't lips eel...even... mmove...

I'm... I'm... I can... Kim, Kim you would have later... *loved* this so, so much. I love...

Love...*look*... look at that sky up there, it's... Ah... and...

and I'm flew...*flying* now...how can be flying...me? Doesn't mu...muc...Mum...*matter*... does it? Does it mu...? Does this any of—

I'm flying again. Oh *God* how I missed... The blue, the clouds...

Oh I God how ...

Oh God...

God... oh—

End recording.

ACKNOWLEDGEMENTS

A huge thank you to Graeme Reynolds at Horrific Tales for his interest in my work, and for wanting to publish this tale – proof that a conversation late at night in a convention pub can lead to some very interesting things... My thanks to Ben Baldwin for yet another cracking cover, and Tim Lebbon for the brilliant introduction.

As usual, hugs and big thanks to all my friends in the writing and film/TV world, for their continuing help, advice and support. You know who you all are. A very special thank you, though, to people like Clive Barker, Neil Gaiman, Stephen Jones, Mandy Slater, Amanda Foubister, Alexandra Benedict, Christopher Fowler, Stephen Volk, Nick Vince, Barbie Wilde, John Connolly, Pete & Nicky Crowther, Simon Clark and so many more there isn't the space to list here; I really wish there was. I never take any of you for granted.

Last, but never, ever least, a big words are not enough thank you to my supportive family – especially my wonderful, wonderful wife Marie. Love you all more than anything.

THANK YOU FOR READING

Thank you for taking the time to read this book. We sincerely hope that you enjoyed the story and appreciate your letting us try to entertain you. We realise that your time is valuable, and without the continuing support of people such as yourself, we would not be able to do what we do.

As a thank you, we would like to offer you a free ebook from our range, in return for you signing up to our mailing list. We will never share your details with anyone and will only contact you to let you know about new releases.

You can sign up on our website

Http://www.horrifictales.co.uk

If you enjoyed this book, then please consider leaving a short review on Amazon, Goodreads or anywhere else that you, as a reader, visit to learn about new books. One of the most important parts about how well a book sells is how many positive reviews it has, so if you can spare a little more of your valuable time to share the experience with others, even if its just a line or two, then we would really appreciate it.

Thanks, and see you next time!

THE HORRIFIC TALES PUBLISHING TEAM

ABOUT THE AUTHOR

Paul Kane is an award-winning writer and editor based in Derbyshire, UK. His short story collections include *Alone (In the Dark)*, *Touching the Flame*, *FunnyBones*, *Peripheral Visions*, *Shadow Writer*, *The Adventures of Dalton Quayle*, *The Butterfly Man and Other Stories*, *The Spaces Between*, *Ghosts* and *Monsters*. His novellas include *Signs of Life*, *The Lazarus Condition*, *RED* and *Pain Cages*. He is the author of such novels as *Of Darkness and Light*, *The Gemini Factor* and the bestselling *Arrowhead* trilogy (*Arrowhead*, *Broken Arrow* and *Arrowland*, gathered together in the sell-out omnibus edition *Hooded Man*), a post-apocalyptic reworking of the Robin Hood mythology. His latest novels are *Lunar* (which is set to be turned into a feature film), the short Y.A. novel *The Rainbow Man* (as P.B. Kane), the sequel to *RED* - *Blood RED* - and *Sherlock Holmes and the Servants of Hell* from Solaris.

He has also written for comics, most notably for the *Dead Roots* zombie anthology alongside writers such as James Moran (*Torchwood*, *Cockneys vs. Zombies*) and Jason Arnopp (*Dr Who*, *Friday The 13th*) and for the Seraphim/Madefire Motion Comic adaptations of *The Books of Blood*. Paul is co-editor of the anthology *Hellbound Hearts* (Simon & Schuster) - stories based around the Clive Barker mythology that spawned *Hellraiser* - *The Mammoth Book of Body Horror*(Constable & Robinson/Running Press), featuring the likes of Stephen King and James Herbert, A CARNIVÀLE *of Horror* (PS) featuring Ray Bradbury and Joe Hill, and *Beyond Rue Morgue* from Titan - stories based around Poe's detective, Dupin.

His non-fiction books are *The Hellraiser Films and Their Legacy*, *Voices in the Dark* and *Shadow Writer* - *The Non-Fiction. Vol. 1 & 2*, and his genre journalism has appeared in the likes of *SFX*, *Fangoria*, *Dreamwatch*, *Gorezone*, *Rue*

Morgue and *DeathRay*. He has been a Guest at Alt.Fiction five times, was a Guest at the first SFX Weekender, at Thought Bubble in 2011, Derbyshire Literary Festival and Off the Shelf in 2012, Monster Mash and Event Horizon in 2013, Edge-Lit in 2014, plus HorrorCon, Liverpool Horror Fest and Grimm Up North in 2015, as well as being a panellist at FantasyCon and the World Fantasy Convention, a judge of Sci-Fi London's Flash Fiction Competition 2016, and co-chair of the UK arm of the Horror Writers Association.

His work has been optioned for film and television, and his zombie story "Dead Time" was turned into an episode of the Lionsgate/NBC TV series *Fear Itself*, adapted by Steve Niles (*30 Days of Night*) and directed by Darren Lynn Bousman (*SAW II-IV*). He also scripted *The Opportunity*, which premiered at the Cannes Film Festival, *Wind Chimes* (directed by Brad "*7th Dimension*" Watson and which sold to TV), *The Weeping Woman* - filmed by award-winning director Mark Steensland and starring Tony-nominated actor Stephen Geoffreys (*Fright Night*) - and *Confidence*, starring *Hellraiser* and *Nightbreed*'s Simon Bamford. You can find out more at his website www.shadow-writer.co.uk which has featured Guest Writers such as Dean Koontz, Robert Kirkman, Charlaine Harris and Guillermo del Toro.

ALSO FROM HORRIFIC TALES PUBLISHING

High Moor by Graeme Reynolds

High Moor 2: Moonstruck by Graeme Reynolds

High Moor 3: Blood Moon by Graeme Reynolds

Of A Feather by Ken Goldman

Whisper by Michael Bray

Echoes by Michael Bray

Voices by Michael Bray

Angel Manor by Chantal Noordeloos

Bottled Abyss by Benjamin Kane Ethridge

Lucky's Girl by William Holloway

The Immortal Body by William Holloway

Wasteland Gods by Jonathan Woodrow

Dead Shift by John Llewellyn Probert

The Grieving Stones by Gary McMahon

The Rot by Paul Kane

COMING SOON

Song of the Death God by William Holloway

High Cross by Paul Melhuish

The Last Veil (Testaments I and II) by Joseph D'Lacey

Other Books by Paul Kane:

Novels

Arrowhead

Broken Arrow

Arrowland

Hooded Man (Omnibus)

The Gemini Factor

Of Darkness and Light

Lunar

Sleeper(s)

The Rainbow Man (as P.B. Kane)

Blood RED

Sherlock Holmes and the Servants of Hell

***Forthcoming*: Deep RED**

Novellas/Novelettes

Signs of Life

The Lazarus Condition

Dalton Quayle Rides Out

RED

Pain Cages

Creakers (chapbook)

Flaming Arrow

The Bric-a-Brac Man

Snow

The PI's Tale

The Crimson Mystery

The Rot

Collections

Alone (In the Dark)

Touching the Flame

FunnyBones

Peripheral Visions

The Adventures of Dalton Quayle

Shadow Writer

The Butterfly Man and Other Stories

The Spaces Between

Ghosts

Monsters

The Dead Trilogy

Forthcoming: **Shadow Casting, Disexistence & Nailbiters**

Editor & Co-Editor

Shadow Writers Vol. 1 & 2

Terror Tales #1-4

Top International Horror

Albions Alptraume: Zombies

The British Fantasy Society: A Celebration

Hellbound Hearts

The Mammoth Book of Body Horror

A Carnivàle of Horror: Dark Tales from the Fairground

Beyond Rue Morgue

Forthcoming: **Dark Mirages**

Paul Kane

Non-Fiction

Contemporary North American Film Directors: A Wallflower Critical Guide (Major Contributor)

Cinema Macabre (Contributor)

The Hellraiser Films and Their Legacy

Voices in the Dark

Shadow Writer - The Non-Fiction. Vol. 1: Reviews

Shadow Writer - The Non-Fiction. Vol. 2: Articles & Essays

Lightning Source UK Ltd.
Milton Keynes UK
UKOW02n1555120916

282815UK00001B/2/P